# MISFIT LIL CLEANS UP

A senseless killing prevents scout and guide Jackson Farraday from investigating an odd situation in the Black Dog mining settlement. So he tricks Lilian Goodnight into spying at the High Meadows cattle ranch. Lil discovers range boss Liam O'Grady running a haywire outfit, crewed by deep-dyed misfits. She then finds she must rescue an ex-British army officer, Albert Fitzcuthbert, from renegade Indians. And Lil faces ever more problems that only her savvy, daring and guns can settle!

CHAP O'KEEFE

# MISFIT LIL CLEANS UP

*Complete and Unabridged*

**LINFORD**
*Leicester*

First published in Great Britain in 2008 by
Robert Hale Limited
London

First Linford Edition
published 2009
by arrangement with
Robert Hale Limited
London

British Library CIP Data

O'Keefe, Chap.
    Misfit Lil cleans up- -
    (Linford western library)
    1. Misfit Lil (Fictitious character)- -Fiction.
    2. Western stories. 3. Large type books.
    I. Title II. Series
    823.9'14–dc22

    ISBN 978–1–84782–852–1

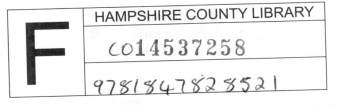
This book is printed on acid-free paper

# 1

## Death at Black Dog

The walls of the saloon were of canvas, dirty brown and stained both in and out. The floor was nothing but stamped dirt, good for absorbing the spills of liquor and the spat streams of chewed tobacco juice. And blood . . .

Hopes rotted away and dreams died within the tent's confines.

Jackson Farraday, the civilian scout, came to the saloon — stepping over pegs and taut guy-ropes to the fly-obscured entrance — in the course of a reconnoitre commissioned by the army. Colonel Brook Lexborough, commander at Fort Dennis, was aware of the possible disturbance to the peace threatened by the saloon, several others of its kind and the mushrooming settlement they served. Peace was fragile in the hinterland of

Lexborough's post.

Jackson looked in. By the saloon's hanging lamps, he saw men he knew must be of all kinds and ages, though a trick of the wan light and the murk of cigarette and pipe smoke reduced faces beyond a few yards to the shapelessness of dough and the greyness of putty.

The few women present were bright and flashy hurdy-gurdy girls, bare-shouldered and short-skirted, employed by the saloon to lure men starved of the softer things in life and to dispense extra fun and favours in parts of the big tent separated off by canvas partitions. Out of sight but not of earshot, these transactions must inflame the envy of those without the ready money to facilitate them and had considerable potential to cause trouble.

The crowd was mostly drunk and noisy. Also frowzy and unwashed.

Jackson was of an opinion the raw camp and tatterdemalion township of Black Dog springing up around it were the creation of unreliable geologists and scheming promoters.

The territory was shunned by legitimate investors, their fingers having been burned badly by the disastrous record of Utah's silver mines in the 1870s, especially the gigantic fraud of the Emma Mine. But a certain breed of rabble was undeterred. When it was heard that Indians were mining lead, silver and gold in a remote mountain canyon, the greedy and ever-hopeful had flocked to the spot to stake out claims.

Black Dog was born, named after the canyon's most possessive prior inhabitant — a vicious, feral beast who barked and snapped endlessly at the intruders and whose one use for the stakes they planted had nothing to do with legal processes. Early in the piece, he was dispatched peremptorily by a prospector's rifle bullet, going to his death untaught in the incomprehensible practices and the might of avaricious man.

'Looking for a poker game, mister?'

'Well, no, I wasn't,' Jackson replied

equably, 'though it's right kind of you.' His accoster, who had come up from behind on quiet feet, evidently hadn't recognized him, though he had him. He savvied his name was Cullen Fowler.

'Pity, that,' Fowler said, buttoning his trousers' front. 'The fellers inside an' me would sure have been glad to have you.'

They went in. Jackson turned his feet to the long bar, which was a series of planks set up on trestles. Fowler pointed himself to a table at the rear where three men awaited him around a card table.

Frowning, Jackson called for whiskey. He was served bad corn liquor of the kind commonly called rotgut. Corn was plentiful and the distillation process simple. The best that could be said for the stuff was that the alcohol content could be relied on to kill germs. He drank reflectively, sipping rather than gulping.

Cullen Fowler had shown up from time to time in this country's better-established town of Silver Vein, which was now more of a ranching centre. He'd professed his calling to be cattle-buying. But he spent much of his days as well his nights around card tables, too, tempting the unwary out of their innocent five- and ten-cent draw poker into high-stakes games.

'How come you buy so few cattle?' a rancher might ask on occasion.

'Contracts are about filled for the season,' Fowler would prevaricate and his eyes would narrow shrewdly. 'I figure we might do a deal for the sake of the game though — your having about lost your shirt an' pants on it. Say, a hundred head next spring to cover the debt, beef prices at roundup time being of no account.'

Jackson had a fair idea Cullen Fowler was more professional gambler than cattle buyer. He sure knew how to fleece his opponents at the tables. Of imposing, intimidating build, he looked like a gorilla dressed in store clothes. But his manners were correct and figuring the thoughts that went on behind the button eyes in his strange, broad-nosed face was ultimately an exercise in supposition.

Nonetheless, Jackson didn't like Cullen Fowler one bit. It seemed to him the deals he made to help out his unlucky 'friends' were at terms decidedly favourable to himself.

As for Fowler's failure to place himself, Jackson Farraday, that — surely — could only be reconciled with the man's total absorption with members of society who had weaknesses he could exploit. And no others.

Jackson wasn't easy to pass over. He was every inch a frontiersman and stood out among Black Dog's very motley company. He was imposingly tall with long, sun-bleached hair and a neat chin-beard.

He also did have a reputation locally, but maybe not amongst the newcomers who'd come to Black Dog from all parts, California diggings to Virginia wheatfields. In the past, he'd hunted buffalo and supplied meat for railroad construction workers. He'd also carried dispatches through hostile Indian country. But he had most in common with the pathfinders who'd blazed western trails earlier in the century.

More than cursory conversation might have revealed, too, that Jackson was an educated man. He reputedly spoke seven languages plus an assortment of Indian dialects. He subscribed to the beliefs of the visionary explorer and lobbyist John Wesley Powell, who promoted scientific survey and the rational use of the West's resources.

In all of these things Fowler presumably had no interest. He'd neglected to learn them, instead cultivating the acquaintance of men who had money from which they could be separated. Right now, one such weaved his way through the throng to Fowler's card game, where the next dealer had gathered up the cards and was tidying them into a pack for his shuffle.

The arrival wasn't another of the mining crowd strangers: he was Liam

O'Grady, a still-youngish man with shoulders a mite stooped from hard work, or maybe the burden of managing the High Meadows ranch for absentee owners. Tall and leanly built, O'Grady's face was handsome in an irregular way. His lips would as readily break into a smile as his dark eyes would be quick to show the flash of temper.

Now what would he be doing here, Jackson asked himself? But it needed no lengthy pondering. Black Dog was closer to the High Meadows headquarters than Silver Vein and O'Grady had always been a sociable type since the days he'd arrived in the territory as a lad, romantically seeking adventure and fortune, and been taken on as a tenderfoot cowboy at Ben Goodnight's Flying G.

O'Grady was older now, married and in a position of responsibility, but the urge for some sort of excitement probably still flowed in his veins. In Black Dog, cares and workaday boredom could be put aside for a while.

'Hey, Cullen! How about letting me

set in your empty chair?' he called.

Fowler nodded. 'Sure enough, feller. No worries on my score. Any time you want.'

Jackson received the hint that the pair had already made acquaintance. He frowned some more. He wondered if O'Grady was aware of Fowler's prowess as a gambler; whether he'd played with and doubtless lost to him before; whether he could still afford to cover his bets tonight.

Jackson's eyes flicked to the centre of the table. Quite a pot, he thought. The pile of chips must amount to several hundred dollars. Would O'Grady be able to buy in, or would he be granted chips through some accommodation with the cattle buyer?

He was too far away through the shifting crowd to catch what happened, but the game got under way.

The man on Fowler's right dealt, the cards flipping smoothly from his fingers. Bidding on the hand seemed to cause no big excitement and the pot passed to one of the miners. The next few hands proceeded.

The O'Grady of old would have taken his losses with equanimity, accepting triumph or disaster without a flicker of an eyelash, maybe even a rueful jest. Not so the O'Grady Jackson saw tonight. When they weren't holding cards, his hands twisted nervously, the one against the other. He swallowed repeatedly and cuffed his brow.

Jackson drew nearer and paid more attention.

The deal went to the man on Fowler's right again. Jackson thought he might be the owner of the Black Dog hardware store. O'Grady wet his lips and opened the betting with a hundred dollars.

The players drew cards, O'Grady drawing three, Fowler one. The others, including the hardware merchant, took a pair each. O'Grady doubled in a jerky voice. Two men decided not to stay, leaving the play to three: O'Grady, the merchant and Fowler.

O'Grady said, 'It's up a hundred.'

'Yours an' two more,' Fowler said.

The hardware man pursed his mouth. 'Make it a further five.'

Behind Jackson, someone took in breath with a gasp. 'God! Another five hundred to stay.'

O'Grady hesitated a second, then he seemed to slump and quiver. He looked more than a man whose nerve had snapped. He was pale and sick. He placed his cards in front of him with a tired gesture of defeat.

He said despairingly, 'This is much too rich for me, gents.' Then, turning to Fowler: 'I can take on no more, Cullen.'

To Jackson's ears, it sounded an enigmatic announcement that called for a response, which it might have received, but never did.

For at that moment, pandemonium broke out.

A newcomer to the saloon, short and stocky, dark-haired like a Welshman and flourishing a short leather whip, made an angry beeline for a lone drinker well into his cups. He was madder than hell. With a roar, he shoved aside bodies that stood in his path.

'Steal me pick and shovels, would ye, eh? Ye dirty, stinkin' squarehead!'

The drinker, a Teutonic type with greasy flaxen hair, promptly hauled an old pistol from a belt hidden under a smelly sheepskin coat.

'I steal noffing, liar! You talk against me. Well, you haf a gun, use it while you haf der chance!'

'I'm no gunfighter!' the Welshman cried.

But the pistol was already waving in the drunk's hand as he rose to his unsteady feet. So the other tried to use his whip. The lash tangled with a bystander who let out a shrill yell.

The pistol in the lurching Teuton's hand blasted. The slug flew wild. It travelled across the tent through the smoke haze, incredibly managing to miss several patrons' heads by fractions of inches, before holing the canvas and whizzing out into the night.

All about Jackson, men ducked and ran.

'Hold your fire!' Jackson bellowed.

But in this lawless place, where authority was properly held by no one, neither man paid his order a jot of notice.

The stocky accuser dropped his whip, drew his firearm, an old Colt Army that had plainly seen many previous owners, and gunman or not, fired twice.

Flame streaked from its muzzle and the second shot hit the startled drunk and spun him round. He pirouetted like a dancer, remarkably kept his balance and ended up facing his enemy once more.

He fired again and this bullet did slam into the man who'd aimed to whip him. It hit him high in the left shoulder and punched him backwards, tottering till he fell on his broad behind.

In reply, the whip man's weapon exploded a third time.

From a sitting position, he shot the

drunk through the chest and the man staggered. Then he was up on his feet and he shot the drunk again, putting him down on to his hands and knees, where he vomited bloodily from mouth and nose.

Before Jackson could reach the man who'd come to right the theft of a pick and shovels, he put a third bullet into his drunken suspect. It went through his head and was instantly fatal.

Jackson chopped the Colt Army from the would-be thief-punisher's grasp and held him prisoner.

The Welshman swore and kicked and struggled with all the might of a desperate, suddenly frightened man. The enormity of killing a man — murdering him — had dawned, giving him the strength of ten despite his wounded shoulder.

'Help me hold him!' Jackson called, but the tent crowd, already depleted, rapidly lit out. In a young mining camp, discretion was the better part of valour. No one wanted to buy into the fatal fight or its future consequences. They had lives to live and fortunes of their own to make. A trial in some rudimentary miners' court would be inconvenient, while its uncertain results might pose danger to those called upon to give evidence as witnesses.

Jackson couldn't keep a grip on the kicking, biting, fist-throwing prisoner. And once he'd broken loose, the man didn't stay to fight. He fled.

No one tried to stop him till he was mounting a saddled horse tied outside.

'Hey! That's my hoss!' the irate owner cried from across the rutted roadway.

'Much obliged!' the skedaddling Welshman responded, and rode off hell-for-leather.

A half-hearted pursuit was organized, but Jackson soon knew it was too late. The killer had outdistanced them, leaving only the smell of his dust, and it was unlikely he'd show his face in the district again.

By the time Jackson was able to turn

his thoughts back to Cullen Fowler, Liam O'Grady and the card game, the players in that episode had also long departed the scene.

But Jackson was still intrigued by what he'd observed. And concerned . . . Something was afoot between the manager cum range boss of the British-owned ranch and the gambling cattle-buyer. But what?

One had a reputation for being a considerate, fair-minded and savvy ramrod, relatively young and holding down a big, demanding job. The other was an impersonal, efficient and calculating businessman with a liking, not to say talent, for gambling at cards, and who was unlikely to grant any favours out of comradeship.

Guesses at what was going on weren't answers, and the latter were what Jackson wanted. He knew O'Grady tolerably well, but not enough to ask questions that might give a proud man offence — or sound like unwarranted intrusion into his private affairs, or, worse, imply an accusation as yet unfounded.

More information was necessary before the taking of interest at a higher level could be justified. He could use the help of a good man who had the time and an existing relationship with High Meadows to exploit as a means to innocent entry . . .

After some thought, he was struck by an overlooked solution to his problem.

His eyes lit up. Of course . . . Misfit Lil!

# 2

## Recruiting Lil

The trusty grey cow-pony standing in the lean-to back of the shack pawed the ground and gave a low whinny.

In the building itself, his owner, a tall, well set-up young woman, dressed mannishly in her favoured garb of fringed buckskin coat and pants, was instantly alert.

'Someone coming, eh, Rebel?' she said softly.

At this time, Miss Lilian Goodnight — or Misfit Lil as she was widely known — had made a temporary home in premises built by an elderly mining engineer. The timbers were hurriedly and roughly hewn and could have done with creosote or pitch for waterproofing and preservation. But the old man had provided his shack with a stove and tin chimney and left a handy stack of firewood for cold nights.

A hopeful jasper, he'd come to the vicinity in search of a silver mine. He'd made claims and charts and drawings and notes, but never realized his dream. Expert knowledge had evidently failed him. When health did likewise, he'd abandoned his project, his spartan home, its basic utensils and its rough-and-ready furnishings, to return East in search of urgent medical attention and a less demanding retirement.

With no one on hand whose permission needed to be sought, Lil had squatted gratefully in the abandoned shack.

On her arrival, it had been in a hell of a mess. A bunch of fugitives had passed through on a route that followed the famed Outlaw Trail — from Montana and Wyoming, down through Utah, and on to Arizona, New Mexico and the convenience of the southern border around El Paso. The outlaws had used and trashed the mining man's old home, leaving chairs and table over-turned, broken china and pots and pans scattered across the floor.

Lil had put the mess to rights and taken up residence. She appreciated the shack's isolation. Off a dizzying mountain pass, only the most inquisitive traveller came across it unexpectedly along a narrow side-trail, nestled amongst tall cottonwood trees.

The lonesomeness was important.

It was very soon after the murderous affair of Major Ezra Creede. Before he'd been stabbed to death with an antique dagger, the hard-eyed, hard-handed major had forced Lil over his knees at a Fort Dennis ball for 'correction' after she'd given sass to a visiting Washington general. He'd turned up the skirt and petticoat she'd been wearing against custom for the grand occasion. Nor to her horror had this been the only preliminary. Callously, he'd also tugged clear to her knees the last-line protection of a ladylike pair of white cotton drawers. Shamefully exposed, she'd

20

been made to look the part of a wanton brat.

Her public spanking had been witnessed by a shocked but deeply interested part of Silver Vein's significant citizenry.

Lil had never been too fussy about her reputation, but she wasn't ready yet to meet eyes that had fixed in fascination on the humiliatingly crimsoned cheeks of her bottom and the other private details of her upended anatomy unavoidably displayed in the course of Creede's rigorous chastisement.

Hence, the wilderness retreat suited her fine for the present. She could exist hermit-fashion, like an old-time mountain man. From an early age, she'd practised woodcraft and the skills of living off the land. She knew the surrounding country — the maze of parched canyons and the desolate, forbidding magnificence of the mountains — as well as a city-bred girl knew her backyard.

And it was here, in her commandeered shack, that the man in the world she admired the most, came to visit her.

'Hullo, the house!' his strong voice called, seconds after Rebel had raised his warning.

'Well, goddamn!' Lil said, with a cheerful grin to herself. 'If it ain't you, Mr Jackson Farraday!'

'I've been looking for you all over,' he said.

Lil scoffed. 'I know that ain't true. You could find me any ol' time you wanted, Jackson.'

Jackson was a tracker of great ability and near legendary repute. He was also her hero, much to his occasional embarrassment and constant misgiving — not because he didn't like her but apparently because he was almost twice her age.

Lil found this ridiculous and regrettable. Her only consolation was that he didn't dismiss out of hand her ambition to become as proficient as himself in all the talents that had made him a top scout, much sought after by the military and others. It made her glow with pleasure whenever he acknowledged she wasn't far short of her objective.

But when he was around, a certain tension was always in the air.

'You shouldn't be out here on your own all the time,' he said, quickly dispelling the warmth of greeting. 'Your self-reliance is impressive, but it's dangerous for a girl.'

Lil laughed ironically, dismissively.

'Where do you suggest I go? In town, I'd come face to face with prim 'n' proper matrons with my other end in their minds! All busting to rush off and disapprove among themselves in whispers . . . comparing notes on what they thought was visible to their knowing eyes at the fort ball. How it was plain I was a slut and suchlike. The hypocrites! Some women cheered Creede on. I heard it. Why did they let it happen? Why did they *look?*'

Jackson said, glum-faced, 'I don't know.'

Lil wasn't finished. 'And in town — most anywhere, point of fact — seeing me again will turn the dragons' menfolk thinking straight off to things aside from a larruping that might be done to a bare-assed girl of lost virtue!'

Jackson swallowed, maybe guiltily. He was familiar enough with her plain-spokenness. Lil guessed he, too, had found Creede's debasing punishment of her as stirring as he'd declared it excessive and inexcusable. He was all male, after all. But Jackson — oh, the pity of it! — chose to act with rectitude, always . . .

Though a girl could do without perverts, she had her needs, and Lil was sorry about Jackson's chosen stance.

'These things have to be forgotten, I agree,' Jackson said.

After a heavy moment's silence, while each communed with only themselves, he brightened and said, 'But you do have friends, Miss Lilian. How would you like to work on a ranch again, like you admired to do before your pa sent you away from the Flying G to Boston? The range-riding, the roping of calves and the driving of cows . . . your skills were the match of any male hand's, they say.'

'They were,' Lil said without modesty. She thought back to her earlier days, long before the Creede episode.

'I could match 'em in cussing and rough-and-tumble, too. There wasn't any real sin, but Pa said the skylarking wasn't fitting for a respectable girl. I was dispatched for education and refinement at a seminary for the daughters of gentlemen. And you know what I did there.'

Nobody in the Silver Vein country needed reminding, she thought, least of all Jackson Farraday. Deprived of the strenuous, physical exercise she was used to, she'd secretly cultivated the forbidden acquaintance of the exclusive Boston academy's handsome gardener's-boy.

After lights-out, she'd shared her

findings — him, too — with her sheltered classmates. Albeit enrolled for semi-classical education and what was called 'finishing', most of the Eastern girls had previously been deterred from natural curiosity in what healthy birds and bees, cattle and humans did. The eager set had commenced extra-curricular studies in a garden shed with blushing yet co-operative course-material.

Adventure! Freedom! The odd *chemise de nuit*, so inconveniently obstructive, was soon being taken off by illicit candle-light so the girls could make examinations and comparisons of themselves and their one male companion. Later, some minor discomfort was borne with fortitude and former maidens of good but restrictive family went on to discover the delicious sensations for which nature had so thought-fully equipped them.

The upshot of the pleasurable exer-tions had been a sniffing-out, an outcry and expulsions. As Lil saw it, she and Boston hadn't hitched up alongside one another at all. Railed back West in disgrace as a ringleader, 'Miss Lilian' had quickly become 'Misfit Lilian' and, after a few more rebellious escapades, simply Misfit Lil.

'So what's this 'meanwhile back at the ranch' foolery?' Lil asked. 'I ain't any more ready to tackle a return to the Flying G than for facing Silver Vein. You want I should crawl back to my despairing dad with abject apologies, you can forget it! Relations stay strained.'

Jackson kept courteous and pleasant. 'I didn't want that you should crawl anywhere. Hard winter coming though. Leaves are browning, might drop sooner this year; antelope heading out of the higher hills early. On top of that, the Black Dog camp's turning rotten. You mightn't be safe here much longer.'

'So just what do you suggest, Mr Farraday?'

The answer was oblique. 'Liam O'Grady was one of your best pals at the Flying G, wasn't he?'

Lil was puzzled, but said, 'Sure, he

was hired on as the youngest hand when I was about twelve. He played the clown like a big brother. But Pa said it was indecent when he caught him partnering me in a wheelbarrow race got up by the crew. I was wearing levis like I always did, so what he figured wrong, I don't know. He'd've gotten real mad if he'd known Liam used to follow me up trees when I still wore skirts and seldom bothered with knickers! Not that Liam would ever have dreamed of abusing the innocence of a kid.'

Jackson groaned in exasperation. 'Must this talk keep turning to impropriety, Miss Lilian?'

Lil was idly amused. 'You're grumbling, Mr Farraday. It's all sounded pertinent and reasonable to me, but I'd be happy to guide conversation someplace else. What were you going to say about Liam O'Grady? Isn't he ramrodding High Meadows these days? Done well for hisself, I hear.'

'I went to see him today,' Jackson said, cutting to the business. 'There's big foreign money behind High Meadows and he's always tolerable busy. Has a place for another hand, I understand, and I suggested you'd be well-suited and likely available.'

'Yeah?' Lil said drily. 'Well, thanks for putting in the good word. I can imagine the tales that'll be told if it gets around a female has shaken out her blankets and made her bed in the High Meadows bunkhouse!'

The Reverend Titus Fisher, Silver Vein's sniffy, full-bearded sky-pilot might find more to say than his customary 'Well I never!' Big-bottomed Miss Purity Wadsworth, president of the local Ladies' Temperance Society, would make sure everybody this side of the Pearly Gates was informed of the latest lapse from morality.

Jackson sighed. 'Nowise would there be a bunkhouse problem. The ranch house where Liam lives with his wife has rooms to spare.'

'I could make do in a hayloft anyhow,' Lil said.

But she'd met Mary O'Grady a few times and wouldn't mind being under the same roof. Mrs O'Grady was a fine, friendly woman. She also happened to bake mouth-watering cookies and cake, the best Lil had ever eaten.

Jackson said, 'You should ride over and hear what Liam has to offer . . .'

Lil drew a deep breath, but became pensive.

She thought of the old, exuberant times at her father's ranch when she'd known little of restraint and her corner of the world had been filled solely by hard-working, hard-playing men. Despite rough dress and ignorance of etiquette, most of them were what she'd later learned to term gentlemen. With their help, she'd developed her talents and acquired her expertise. For instance, she'd become a crack-shot with a Colt — her pa's cowboys had been first to call her the 'the Princess of Pistoleers' — and as at home in the saddle as on foot or wagon wheels.

'Maybe I will,' she said, after a long moment's reflection. 'I'm all mixed up nowadays, but it was fun when Liam was at the Flying G. To boot, he appreciated I was a real cowgirl.'

She remembered the days that had all seemed perfect — blue-skied and spring-like with only fleecy white clouds and a sun that rose and fell in a regular blaze of splendour; when there were convivial camp-fires in a chuck wagon's shadow at roundup time, and uncritical friends who sang plaintive songs by night to calm a herd that couldn't know the words were frequently bawdy substitutes for the original lyrics. It was a measure of her acceptance by the cowboys that they'd felt no requirement to moderate language or behaviour when she was around. Lil abhorred inhibitions — no way could she entertain being one herself.

So she added, 'But I wouldn't want to make Liam any trouble.'

'You won't be making him any trouble,' Jackson said keenly. 'Not a bit. Why, a smart girl like you might be just the person to keep an eye open for any

trouble that might threaten him; anything strange going on.'

'What do you mean?'

He lifted a shoulder and tilted his
head of long, loose hair. 'Oh, nothing
particular, I guess, but the High Meadows
prime stock could be considered rich
pickings for rustlers and other buzzards.'

There were no flies on Lil. She knew
he was hiding something from her and
was doubly intrigued.

Here was a touch of mystery, the like
of which could almost be guaranteed to
seize her attention. If the O'Gradys were
in some sort of bother, she'd be mighty
proud to stand by them. Moreover, she
always relished fighting a good fight!

And the chance of making reports to
Jackson — of being useful in his eyes
— was irresistible. Maybe, just maybe,
if she fulfilled his expectations, he
might at last find her worthy of a more
special friendship . . .

She came quickly to a resolve to take
up Jackson's suggestion and Liam
O'Grady's invitation.

# 3

## Trouble on High Meadows

From a distance, Misfit Lil saw Mary O'Grady on the veranda of the High Meadows ranch house and waved.

Mary lifted her hand from the white-painted rail and returned the gesture. Lil urged Rebel into a canter for the last few hundred yards of trail to the ranch buildings, which were on rising ground and surrounded by lush grassland. The horse, which she'd known all his life, caught the lightness and confidence of her spirit, and came up to the house jauntily.

Liam O'Grady's wife was a good handful of years Lil's senior, comely in a mature way, being bigger at the bosom and wider at the hips. With her shimmering eyes and an unconscious sensuousness, the best single word for

Mary was generous.

'Why, howdy, Lil!' she greeted her. 'What brings you riding our way?'

Lil swung down from the saddle lithe and easy.

'Jackson Farraday tells me Liam needs an extra hand. He wasn't stringing me, was he?'

That seemed to amuse Mary.

'Oh, I don't think Mr Farraday would put anyone wrong,' she said, shaking her blonde head. 'Least of all you! No, High Meadows has a call for good 'punchers. And I figure it'd please myself to have you here, too. Lord, O'Grady presently has such a devilish tough crew about the place it'd do me a power of good to see an open and honest face such as your'n!'

'A tough bunch, huh?' Lil mused. 'In what wise tough?'

Mary was not laughing now.

'Well, they sure don't know much about working cattle. More like the wolf and coyote breed you see riding the outlaw trail. Desperadoes. They're some

34

quick with the Colt and act like they own the earth. Hell could be about to pop purty soon!' She turned completely sombre. 'Fact is, I don't know it's rightly safe around here for O'Grady to hire on a — anyone new . . . '

Lil said stoutly, 'If the set-up's good enough for you, it is for me. But why did Liam take on the riff-raff?'

Mary was uncharacteristically evasive. 'Maybe he was given no options. Please don't ask me any questions.'

Lil thought that strange, but she was also anxious to establish herself here and meet the challenge she sensed, so she wasn't prepared to argue the point. Already it was more evident than before that there were a number of things Jackson hadn't told her.

She learned that Liam had ridden into Silver Vein on business and wasn't expected back before nightfall. Mary made her at home, and she caught only brief glimpses of a couple of the hands over to the corrals. To Lil, they didn't look anything much: bandy-legged loudmouths loafing in the sun most of the time, chewing tobacco and swapping brags, though they were ostensibly engaged in breaking horses.

'It's a waste of effort anyways and they should know it,' Lil muttered, though Mary was taking little notice. 'A bronco buster would savvy straight off those animals are owl heads — they'll never be trained to work or to ride.'

Later, Liam O'Grady returned from Silver Vein, coming into the ranch house parlour, clutching a sheaf of papers. They included several that looked like they might be the copies of messages scribbled down on sheets of flimsy paper by the operator at the telegraph office as he took them off the wire.

Liam was scowling, but his eyes brightened at the sight of his handsome wife, who was welcoming loveliness and warm vitality in every line and curve. He tossed the papers on the table, his curly-brimmed stetson to a peg on a wall rack, and embraced her.

'And I see we have company, Mary!' he exclaimed. 'Have you come to sign on, Lil?'

Lil said she had.

His worried, somehow sad face broke in a smile. Handsome, leanly built, he'd always had lips quick to smile just as he had dark eyes quick to show the fire of his temper.

'In truth, I savvy nothing more'n why you don't want to go back to your pa's or into town. But I'll be glad to have you on High Meadows. I've always liked you, Lil, and appreciate you'll pull your weight and be useful.'

He stuck out a calloused hand and they shook.

Lil knew, too, where she stood with Liam O'Grady. He'd done well for himself since he'd given up riding for her father's brand. In those days, aside from their sharing in the general fun of the Flying G, Liam had kept his eyes on her skills and off her girlish attractions. Apart from telling her once or twice she was awful pretty, he'd stuck to business and passed on tips that had tightened her grasp of the fundamentals of ranch work. Though Lil knew Jackson Farraday was into some deeper game, she aimed to repay Liam to the best of her ability.

She excused herself quickly, giving husband and wife the privacy they were due.

When the rest of O'Grady's crew drifted into the ranch headquarters, dishevelled and sweaty, Lil was as unimpressed as Mary. They were the drifter kind at best. Some were shifty-eyed, suggesting craftiness and lobo cunning; others were gloomy and taciturn.

The signs were on all of them of coarse living. Several bore the scars of old fights. Not square fights either. Lil reckoned their fighting would be of the dirty kind — eye-gouging, rabbit-punching, ear-twisting, head-butting. She couldn't imagine them doing range work. They might laze, bungle or bluff their way through winter, but when spring came, and it was time for cutting-out and branding, these *hombres* would be useless. In the noise, dust and confusion of that operation, every man had to know his work thoroughly and do it in a methodical way.

'Huh, the only place in cattle country where these fellows would look in place would be decorating the limb of a cottonwood tree,' Lil commented quietly, darkly.

O'Grady bristled, but because it was from her, he let it go. She knew from his worried frown when he'd introduced her over at the cookhouse, where the crew ate, that he'd noticed those men who'd regarded her at all did it with smirks and all the wrong kinds of interest.

Right then Lil determined that in due course she'd show the swaggering bucks what was what.

Come break of day, Lil was up and carrying a towel and soap to wash herself under the pump back of the ranch house. A smell of bacon drifted from the house.

Lil was thinking how the bacon and beans would go down well with some of Mary's mouth-watering biscuits, all chased with black coffee, when one of the crew stole up on her.

There was no other word than 'stole' for it. The backyard was away from the bunkhouse, relatively secluded, and it was evident from the towel and soap that she'd gone there for private purposes. A gentleman wouldn't intrude.

'What are you looking for, mister?' she asked sharply.

'You, girlie,' the man said, showing himself from behind bushes.

He was solidly built with a barrel torso and legs like a pair of tree trunks. He had a mean, pockmarked face, framed by shaggy hair that was a dirty ginger. She'd heard his pards call him Red. She guessed his colouring had faded some since he'd been given the moniker.

'I know your breed,' he went on. 'Yuh don't fool me none with those men's duds yuh're wearin'. An' I don't give a hang fer this cowgirl rep O'Grady was sellin' the boys. Yuh're jest another li'l trail whore. Yuh'll stick around a coupla days an' empty the suckers' pockets afore yuh ride on. Waal, I figger I'm gonna have me a preview right now — fer free! I'll scrub your back. Haw, haw!'

He was menacing — a mass of unlovely flesh and muscle with a wet tongue running over thick lips between stubbled cheeks and chin. He smelled, too, of horses and cattle overlaid by the odour of his own unwashed body.

'You *what* — !' Lil was more scandalized by his gall than afeared by his threatening tone.

'Yuh heard, sister, git on with the strippin' off an' the washin' down.'

Lil was without gunbelt and unarmed. She could scream for the O'Gradys, but it might also bring this brute's pards at a run, sensing sport, and cause trouble for her new employers. And it would likely spell a quick end to her job and her unspoken mission for Jackson Farraday.

She would have to disabuse Red of his dirty notions some other way.

'Nice friendly guys, your bunch,' she said. 'Make a body feel right flattered and welcome.'

And she strode toward the pump. A heavy zinc pail sat beneath it. She grabbed it up by the handle and swung it as Red came after her, thinking she'd capitulated.

He was hit in the upper chest and face. But the clanging blow had next to no effect. The heavy man gave his shaggy head a shake, blinked his watering eyes and let out a rumble of rage like a prodded bull.

Lil knew then she was going to have a hard time fighting him off single-handed.

He came at her, swinging a ham-like right fist designed to knock her into senseless submission. Lil dodged, grabbed the thug's shirt, and rammed home a punch of her own. It was like hitting a rock.

She was in real trouble. Turn her back, try to run, and she'd be caught and done for before she'd gone two steps. She'd never get away.

The shirt tore from her fingers, which was maybe as well. Backstepping, she weaved and ducked.

'Come here, girlie!' Red growled. 'Come into my arms! This is it — your big chance!'

Red's great arms reached out and seized Lil in a vicious bear-hug.

'Come here! Come an' git it, sweetheart! This is it! This is the time!'

He almost crooned his revolting message.

She felt as though every bone in her body was being crushed. Uselessly, she delivered a couple of short, frantic punches to Red's face, but the grip never slackened. His laughter filled her flaring nostrils with dog's-breath smell.

The sheer weight of Red's bulk forced Lil to the ground. Heart racing, she knew she couldn't let him get on top of her. Once he had her pinned down, the fight would be finished. She rolled, dragging him with her.

They went over and over, grunting and spitting out the dust thrown up around them in gritty clouds.

Lil fought with all her might, but she felt her strength ebbing under the impact of the man's slaps and from wrenching loose of the painful holds he tried to put on her.

Realizing she had to do something decisive, and quickly before she lost her senses, Lil summoned every last vestige of fight she had left. She lifted her knee and drove it into her attacker's crotch.

Red doubled up in agony and went over on to his side.

Free of his bruising, crushing bulk, Lil scrambled to her feet.

Yet with surprising speed of recovery, Red heaved himself up, too, groaning and mouthing curses. He lumbered forward to make another grab.

Lil was panting with exhaustion but, always an interested observer of rough-and-tumble in the largely male world she'd inhabited, she recalled suddenly a move she'd once seen made in a wrestling match at a carnival in Green River.

It was one of those memories that come to mind in the fullest clarity only in moments of great stress. A slim, near-beaten black fighter had faced a white man-mountain near twice his girth. Not only had he won the contest, he'd left his opponent with a permanently crippling back injury.

If her strength held out, if she could calculate the niceties of position and balance, she might just be able to pull off the same feat. It was a chance — maybe her only one.

But even while she was rapidly thinking, Red gave her a swift cuff to the side of her face which sent her spinning backwards round the corner of a watering trough.

She crouched there, trembling a little, shaking her head to try to clear it. She wiped the back of a hand across her bleeding mouth.

Close to the ground, Lil waited for Red to storm after her, powerful, broken-nailed hands reaching out surely for a final time . . . to claim his stunned prize.

# 4

## The Sleepers

Lil was playing a dangerous game of possum. Red came at her full-tilt — a huge, 200 pounds plus of angry man.

'I have yuh, yuh dirty slut!'

Then, rising abruptly, Lil butted her head sharply into the pit of his stomach, and seized his wrist, causing him to pitch forward over her turned and bent back.

With a gigantic heave, Lil straightened up and tossed Red right over her shoulder, harnessing the unstoppable velocity of his own charge.

The man turned a spectacular somersault in the air. His back crashed down so hard on the edge of the trough that the lumber splintered and his head and most of his body went into the water, slopping it over the sides every which way.

And Red screamed.

'She's broke m'back! She's kilt me!'

Men came running, barefoot and pulling on top clothing. Amid cries of shock and bewilderment, the moaning bully was lifted from the trough. He was in a bad way, but Lil didn't think she had broken his back.

'What happened, gal?' someone demanded of her.

'He attacked me and ended up in the water.'

'How in hell . . . ?'

'A Cornish miner in Green River told me something like it was called a flying mare where he came from.'

'Yuh mean, yuh *threw* him?'

'Naw . . . ' Lil said. She shrugged and opened her hands innocently. 'I guess he kind of flew over my shoulder in his hurry.'

Red sobbed. He'd split his scalp and blood as well water dripped from his straggling locks of ginger hair.

'Ah, Gawd! The whore tricked me. She's quick — slippery an' cunnin' as a rattler!'

Leaning against the trough, he looked like the etching of a beached whale Lil had seen in a book.

One of the crew said, 'Your back ain't broke, Red. More like the gal's kinda put somethin' out.'

'Will yuh shuddup? Jest shuddup!'

The hardcases kept on leering a mite incredulously, but Lil sensed their interest in, or their opposition to, a female dressed like an old-time mountain man joining the High Meadows payroll was in most instances now tempered by a wary respect.

Lil wasn't quite sure about the disabling of Red. Did he matter? Had she done the right thing? Would his bleak-eyed, thin-lipped sidekicks fix her in retaliation?

When she returned to the ranch-house kitchen, Mary said tentatively, 'Maybe it's not such a good idea getting hired. Why not ride on right now? You can't trust any of those roughnecks.'

Lil frowned. A good argument could be put up in favour of quitting before she got properly started. Red, she reasoned, was a worthless creature, a nobody existing on the edges of lawful life like scum rimming a pool of water. She couldn't spare him any regrets. He'd got his needings and didn't count in Lil's estimation.

But he was only one of a whole crew of no-accounts. All of Liam O'Grady's men looked the type that lived how and as they could without doing any really honest work. As cowpokes, they spelled only trouble. It was a mystery all right. She meant to get to the bottom of it. The die had been cast when she'd left the engineer's mountain shack.

'Damned if I'll be spooked by bad lots! Isn't it dangerous having men like Red around? He'd've deserved to be hog-tied and whipped if he'd had his way with me. Why has Liam picked so' — she paused — 'shifty-eyed a crowd?'

Mary became defensive. 'Liam spends

more time in Black Dog than Silver Vein. It's closer, and those are the men such a place attracts. The cattle buyer Cullen Fowler prefers the social life of the mining camp, too, and I think Red Ballinger and the rest were recommended by him.'

Lil didn't contest the inadequate explanation. She fell silent, keeping her thoughts to herself. To her mind, Cullen Fowler was a Johnny-come-lately in the district who was more a leech on boom-town life than a genuine cattle businessman. He liked card-playing — as did Liam O'Grady — and there was plenty of that in hastily thrown-up Black Dog; usually in the ubiquitous saloons where myriad forms of gambling and pleasure-taking thrived unchecked, spurred by high-priced bad liquor and attracting undesirables of every stripe.

It was poor judgement on Liam's part to have taken advice from Fowler, hiring for his outfit the worst of drifter trash.

Mary broke a long silence.

'Your boldness will land you in serious trouble one day, Lil, but I'll be pleased to have your company here, I have to admit. And the crew is only half High Meadows's problems.'

Lil's ears pricked up, eager to hear the other half.

'How's that?'

'I'm sure O'Grady won't mind you knowing. It's going to come out soon anyhow. You know that High Meadows is other people's property, don't you?'

Lil nodded. 'Sure. Liam acts as the manager and ramrod for a foreign corporation, doesn't he?'

She was nothing if not thoroughly informed in all aspects of her world. Her knowledge thus extended beyond practical skills. She was aware the range-cattle industry attracted capitalists from not only the East but the old countries, too. The prospect of quick wealth tempted many an Englishman or Scot to invest in huge land purchases and great herds of longhorns. In

England, a parliamentary committee had reported a thirty-three per cent return to stock-owners. It was no big wonder some of the largest cattle companies operating in America were owned by British financiers, keen to make money raising cows they never saw.

The process was similar to the injections of British capital that helped build railroads.

Mary said, 'Yes, High Meadows is owned by a syndicate of foreign investors. And they're not happy with the small profits Liam has been making.'

The ranch wife crossed to a rocker and took up from the seat papers that had been partly hidden by the sewing she'd left there. She handed them to Lil.

'These include the messages Liam brought back yesterday from the telegraph office in Silver Vein.'

Lil scanned the pages, written in the firm pencil strokes of the clerk's hand.

'You can see how it is, Lil . . . the British financiers are plumb tired of waiting for their profits. They figure their American underlings — mainly O'Grady — have bungled with High Meadows. That they might have been cheated.'

'Surely that can't be true!'

'No! I swear my Liam is the victim of circumstances. We've been forced to sell breeding animals and the poorer stuff at low prices, while prime stock has been driven off — probably rustled. But no one has seen anything, found anything.'

Lil showed no surprise on this count. 'Given the hands Liam has, I can believe it. Not a tracker among 'em, I'd bet. Outlaws and Angry-fist's Indian renegades could be stealing High Meadows blind.'

With Mary filling in the gaps left by the telegrams in her slim, strong fingers, Lil made mental notes furiously and soon had the whole black picture.

'So the corporation's bosses are sending their agent in New York, an ex-British Army man' — she checked the name — 'this Major Fitzcuthbert, to check up on High Meadows personally, go over the books and report on what has gone wrong.'

Mary said grimly, 'We've done all we can. Albert Fitzcuthbert might turn out to be a perfectly reasonable man, of course, but it's a mighty big worry for us. And what happens at High Meadows isn't the half of it. Liam has had all manner of details to attend to for the major's comfort.'

'Comfort? Hah! Don't sound like any ex-army man I'd want to know. Can't this Fitzcuthbert shift for himself?'

'Oh,' Mary continued, in a voice that was weary with the problem, 'I should have mentioned that the major will be accompanied by his wife, who I figure isn't accustomed to the rigours of frontier living.'

Lil's eyebrows shot up.

'An English lady! Why, the poor woman! What would she want with inspecting a cattle ranch?'

Mary said slowly, 'I'm not sure, but it seems Major Fitzcuthbert insists she accompanies him everywhere.'

Lil snorted.

'That makes it more ridiculous than ever! How old is this ex-major, and how long has he been married to his wife? I should have thought service life would have made them used to the odd spell of separation.'

'I can't be more forthcoming, on account of we know very little 'bout their private lives,' Mary said.

As nearly as Lil could tell from her tone, Mary also considered it no one's business to pry further.

'Well,' she said. 'That's it then, isn't it? Now, Mary, the bacon I can smell has my mouth watering!'

But as she helped to lay the breakfast table, Lil mused that things had begun to get curiouser and curiouser. She permitted herself a secret, wicked grin and resolved to add the Fitzcuthberts to the list of High Meadows mysteries she aimed to get to the bottom of.

★ ★ ★

Sensing relations with the rest of the HM hands could be a mite soured by her decisive dispatch of Red Ballinger's bid to stamp his brand on her hide, Lil asked Liam O'Grady's permission to look over the scenery alone.

Liam stroked his chin a moment, thinking it over before he answered.

'Yep. It'll give the hotheads a chance to cool down.'

'Much obliged, Liam,' she said. 'I'd like to reacquaint myself with your southern range.'

'I suspect there's been considerable — uh — irregularity going on in that direction lately,' Liam replied, and Lil thought she detected a nervousness in his voice. 'The boys tell me they ain't seen nothing amiss, but allowing for natural growth, herd size was down some at the last roundups — fall and spring both.'

★ ★ ★

Rebel was restive, anxious to be up and going. Lil wheeled him and set out at a gallop.

The best chance to get a view of the country was to follow the top of a ridge, and after several miles of energetic riding, Lil reined in her puffed mount for a breather. Below her stretched a long, grassy meadow, winding through timber like a snake. She spotted several calves or yearlings, grazing unaccompanied.

She guided Rebel down off the ridge, through the timber, to examine them at closer quarters. And she frowned as she went. Maybe I'm over-suspicious, but this bunch of young stuff doesn't look right, she thought.

Her doubts about the rightness of matters were quickly confirmed. The cattle spooked and scattered at her approach, some into the timber. She slipped out a small brass telescope she carried in a pants pocket. She adjusted the lens and was able to see all she needed. They'd stuck up their ears

— enquiring-like, obligingly — at her intrusion into their lonely domain.

Most of the creatures had ear-cuts but were unbranded.

'Sleepers!' Lil exclaimed grimly.

At best, the finding suggested what she'd already summed up. The HM crew was incompetent — lazy, hasty, careless or a combination of all three. At worst, it might be implied something crooked was going on.

'Punchers created sleepers as a second resort. The number of calves that escaped roundup could be large if circumstances — or nefarious choice — dictated. Later, a cowboy would come across an unbranded calf with its branded mother. If he had a stamping iron in his saddle gear, he might brand the calf. If not, or if it was inconvenient to make a branding fire, he could notch or otherwise cut the calf's ears so they matched its mother's. The distinctive earmark was usually registered with a stock owner's brand. The brand could be added to the earmarked beast — a so-called 'sleeper' — at the next roundup.

But the ear-cutting system was open to abuse. Lil's father, Ben Goodnight, was one of the many cattlemen who disapproved strongly of the practice. The reasons were obvious. Opportunity existed for a maverick hunter or a rustler to drive off sleepers and, after altering the ear slits and crops, to brand them with his own or some unknown brand. While the calf was accompanied by its correctly branded and earmarked mother, the discrepancy and the subterfuge would be detected immediately. But not afterwards. For once the calf was weaned, and had attained fuller growth or been forcibly separated from its mama, there was no plain evidence to point to whom it had originally belonged.

Lil saw too many HM sleepers on this range. It went against her grain to accept the situation.

'Just ain't tolerable,' she fretted. 'Liam could have all those critters go missing real easy.'

Shortly after, she turned Rebel. Still thinking her troubled thoughts, she sought out the trail home and pushed back toward the HM headquarters.

'What's wrong?' Liam asked, when she rode into the yard and he came hustling from the house.

'Sleepers,' Lil said with abrupt gruffness. 'Is it High Meadows's policy to let 'em run in astonishing numbers?'

Liam's bronzed face may have paled a smidgeon. He certainly looked uneasy.

'Well — no, 'course not, Lil,' he said huskily. 'But yeah, I'd noticed a few. Not anything suspicious, y'understand. Cattle done well this season.'

'Then why aren't they branded, Liam? Don't your 'punchers know how to rope and throw?'

'Sure they do! And every man swears black and blue he branded every calf he had a rope on last spring.'

'Hmm! Seems strange to me . . . '

'Now don't go biting off more than you can chew, Lil. Leave the worrying

61

to me. These matters can't always be helped, you know. Let it go.'

A strange light came into her eyes, but she nodded and, poker-faced, led her horse away to the barn. She off-saddled and, ankle-deep in the straw, rubbed down Rebel with a piece of burlap, raking the grey's glistening flanks with long sweeps of her powerful arms.

What did Liam O'Grady's acceptance of his lobo crew and its plainly lying word signify? No wonder High Meadows was in trouble and its absentee owners peeved!

She might be liable to bite off more than she could chew at that.

After all, wasn't that Misfit Lil's way?

# 5

## Coach Chase

A blazing hot, enervating day and a train's passenger car — one of three clattering and swaying along behind a brass-trimmed, glossy black locomotive with a smoke-belching diamond-stack — brought Major Albert Fitzcuthbert and his wife, Cecilia, to Green River.

Green River was a railroad town, run by the Denver & Rio Grande Western Railway. Transportation dominated the town's commerce since it was the area's major shipping point for livestock and mining equipment and supplies.

The Fitzcuthberts disembarked.

The ex-British Army man was sixty if he was a day, but he carried himself strongly, imperiously. He wore a top hat, had a showy moustache and bushy side-burns but no beard. On his left

63

coat front, alongside the wing of the lapel, was a row of colourfully beribboned campaign medals with engraved clasps — all shiny, precious or semi-precious metals and bands of red, white and purple fabric.

Under his right armpit, he tucked a stick, his uplifted hand gripping its end which was topped with a silver cap bearing a military insignia. Perhaps the alien length of rattan enabled him to depict himself as still an officer and gentleman, but to the Western loafers at the railroad depot the touch looked plumb silly, without purpose.

'Mebbe the cane's fer walkin',' one conjectured. 'Tho' he don't look like he needs none, seein' as he has two straight-enough laigs . . . '

'Mebbe he'll hit yuh wi' it, Cranky Bill!' the critic's grinning companion joshed.

Mrs Fitzcuthbert appeared only as a mystery to the folks of Green River. Despite the unseasonable heat of the late summer's day, she was travelling in an enveloping cloak of dark hue with hat to match, and was closely veiled.

The couple was directed to the office of the stage-coach line that operated the run to Silver Vein.

'Hurry along, my dear!' Fitzcuthbert ordered. 'We shouldn't be out in this damnably broiling sun at noon. It wouldn't be tolerated in the Punjab. The natives would provide shade for a memsahib.'

The wife said nothing. She clutched and hoisted her skirts clear to her shapely ankles and hastened daintily shod feet to obey his urging.

The watchers took note that the English traveller received a husband's due respect. It was as it should be: his lordly tone brooked no argument; his woman was submissive and compliant as befitted a well-bred wife.

The afternoon stage was readied promptly. Mail was locked in the strongbox under the driving seat. The Fitzcuthberts were installed inside and their bags, along with some freight, secured on the railed top.

The whip climbed to the high driving seat, stood on the footboard and yelled, 'Git goin', hosses!' He cracked the long whip over six pairs of twitching ears, the team lunged into its collars, and the lightly laden coach rolled.

At a smart run, the stage swept out of town, past the railroad company's engine house and its switching yards criss-crossed with iron track.

Leather curtains flapped in the glassless window frames. The coach's interior could accommodate nine passengers with ease, albeit with less comfort than a train car, but the English pair were the sole occupants.

The hot-headed renegade Angry-he-shakes-fist and his bunch of Indian reservation defectors were currently known to be in the vicinity. Also to be on the rampage for spoils and blood . . . Travel was therefore undertaken only for the most urgent reasons or by the adventurous and foolhardy.

Cecilia Fitzcuthbert abandoned her

stoicism in the rocking, hot, dusty and rattling conveyance. From behind the veil, a voice spoke up filled with uncertainty, doubt and trouble.

'Oh, my goodness! Persons must be bounced in such carriages till they're black and blue! Mercy, sir! Did you have to bring me to this horrible West?'

'Be quiet, woman!' Fitzcuthbert snapped. 'You know you're far too valuable to let out of my sight.'

Outside, the country that flashed past was mostly bare and bleak, dotted with occasional trees, stunted cedars and sage.

Fitzcuthbert produced a hip flask of brandy and took a generous gulp. His thoughts, or the liquor, seemed to mellow him.

'With firmness, the cattle company's business will soon be settled. Even here — more *particularly* here — I shall find time to indulge my pleasures. Games of chance flourish in all the West's centres, I'm told. You shall see — there will be an exciting, jovial side to these raw communities.'

'For a man, but what will there be for me?' The question spilled from lips that trembled with its daring.

'You? Why, you may learn to enjoy performing your marital duties better!'

She knew as soon as her last words had left her lips that it had been a mistake to provoke him, but a sense of inequality had got the better of her. Hot all over, she said meekly, 'You have the upper hand, sir, and I cannot change my lot.'

Fitzcuthbert nudged and pinched her, and laughed nastily when she drew away from him.

'Hah! A woman must respect her marriage vows! I'd advise you, young madam, to cultivate doing honour to your master, or it will be the worse for you! You'll find no shoulders to cry on in these parts.'

She turned her head from him silently and shrank into the furthest corner of the seat. Unperturbed, he poked at her with his swagger-cane, pushing the cloth of her skirts deeply into her lap.

At the cry of hurt protest she couldn't suppress, he laughed again.

★ ★ ★

Misfit Lil spotted a rolling dust ball at a distance of several miles on the borders of the High Meadows range. It was coming her way and she knew it would be the afternoon stage on the road from Green River to Silver Vein.

She'd learned previously that today would mark the coming of Major Fitzcuthbert, whose arrival in the country was awaited with a deal of worry by the O'Gradys. Lil had never lacked for curiosity. On impulse, she decided to see if she might glimpse the ominous English agent and the wife he evidently never let leave his side.

She set Rebel at a canter on a course across the rolling range that would intersect the stage road close to the dust cloud.

'Yes, siree, we must go take ourselves a look-see!'

It seemed crazy to her that a man said to have experienced bloody action in hostile corners of the world should want to bring a lady accustomed to the civilized society of European and Eastern cities to Silver Vein and High Meadows. This was no country for her kind, that was a fact. Only the likes of dashing Lieutenant Michael Covington, at Fort Dennis, would figure otherwise.

Mike — how he hated her calling him by that friendly diminutive! — was forever carping at Lil's deficit of refinement and genteel manners. His education, which included a spell at West Point, had left him convinced an angelic decorum was the desirable goal for all good women, not excepting those brought to or raised on the world's wildest frontiers.

Did Fitzcuthbert, a much older man but also of military background, share his fool notions, his delusions?

But Lil was given no time to muse. For an urgent development claimed all her attention.

On the stage trail's straight path to Silver Vein, it passed close to a series of buttes rising brown and mauve from the more level land. From the shadowy cover behind the first emerged a line of half-naked, bronze-skinned riders — Angry-fist and his renegades, the loose ends of dirty headband ties and breech-clouts flying in the breeze . . .

Lil stepped up Rebel's canter to a gallop, then — as the rebel Indians' intentions became clear — to a dead run. They were planning on jumping the coach!

She drew a Colt and fired in the air. The half-dozing man riding shotgun on the stage jerked to full alert and saw her. She pointed to the Indians pounding up to take the stage unawares from behind.

From there, the chase was on.

The coach driver gave his teams the lash, shifting them into a pace that would use them up long before they'd outstrip the Indians' fleet and wiry mustangs.

Hotfoot on the warpath, Angry-fist's men loosed arrows and fired their carbines at the hurtling coach, determined to force it to a standstill. The shotgun guard's Winchester cracked in reply repeatedly.

But hitting moving targets when in motion is a rare feat. Though several feathered arrows soon jutted from the baggage and panelling of the coach as it bounced over a surface too uneven for such speed, no one scored a fatal hit.

Lil wasn't fooled that the stage's situation was anything less than desperate. The Apache party was dedicated to its business. It would dog the whitemen's coach till the horses' stamina gave out.

Lil kept up on a parallel, converging course. She feared the mad pursuit was going to end in ghastly, bloody tragedy.

Angry-fist — one-fisted since his memorable tomahawk duel with Jackson Farraday, frustrated by his handicap and eager for the kill — screeched orders at his riders. His snarling, darkened face was livid and terrible.

One brave drew ahead of his red brothers, got alongside the stage teams and swerved, guiding his small, fast mount with his knees. He rode straight-backed and aimed his carbine at the near lead horse.

He let out a blood-curdling triumphant yell, sure he couldn't miss his target and that the coach would be brought to a crashing halt.

But his confidence was premature. Angling in on him out of the boiling, dirty-white dust cloud of his own making came Misfit Lil. Her Colt was in her fist and she fired.

The buck with the carbine went down as though struck by lightning. The stage rocketed on, jagged flints flying from under its spinning wheels.

The Apaches howled in dismay at the downing of their fleetest rider, but the pursuit was not over, only momentarily checked. Streaming round their fallen comrade and his loose horse, they stormed on.

Adopting Indian tactics herself, Lil quickly slipped one foot out of the stirrup, and swung down along the flank of her racing grey that was away from the red devils. Her precaution was unnecessary. If the Indians gave pause to avenge their shot warrior, their fire went way wide.

Lil cursed. Angry-fist was determined to nail his quarry. Only in a dime novel did a lone white man — or girl — stand the faintest chance of stopping a fast-moving band of marauding 'Paches. No doubt they reckoned on tracking and seizing her at their leisure when they'd accomplished their fiendish designs for the stage, its occupants and contents.

Bravely, she put Rebel on to the stage road and galloped in futile pursuit of the coach and its tormenters. She was convinced the coach was lost.

Accordingly, her thoughts were darkening from black to the blackest when reason for fresh hope was kindled. From behind another of the several buttes, a short column of horsemen advanced. Sun glinted on rifles and brightened the blue of uniforms.

The cavalry!

Immense relief flooded through Lil. The officer in the lead saw the careering coach and its yelling string of pursuers. The detachment swept forward at a gallop.

Rifles cracked viciously, stopping renegade riders dead in their tracks. Several toppled from their mounts, letting out shrieks of shock and pain. Their small, half-wild mustangs milled before stampeding in terror, taking others that became uncontrollable with them.

Angry-fist and the more disciplined remnants of his predatory band hauled up, hesitated momentarily, then wheeled and made off, riding like mad in scattering clouds of dust that obviated chances of rounding them up.

The stage went on another mile, pitching and swaying, before its horses ran out of strength and could be brought to a head-hanging standstill, trembling and lathered with a foam of sweat.

The coach itself was partly off the roadway, slewed at a crazy angle, almost capsized. Misfit Lil reached it moments before the patrol from Fort Dennis.

'Is everyone all right?'

The driver mopped his brow with a yellow kerchief. 'Me an' Abner's a mite discomposed, but unscratched. We ain't seen them varmints till yuh fired your pistol. It was a damn close call.'

The shotgun guard had jumped down and was helping out the two Fitzcuthberts.

'Passengers are considerable shook up, I shouldn't wonder,' he offered.

The returning troopers jogged up, having abandoned the futile bid to run down the surviving raiders. The young officer in charge, surprisingly spick and span, doffed his hat to the Fitzcuthberts.

'Sir! Ma'am! Lieutenant Michael Covington at your service. I'm glad we happened along when we did.'

Lil felt irritated though she couldn't

put her finger on just why. Mike Covington's manner was thoroughly correct, of course, so maybe it was his pleased-as-a-puppy demeanour that grated. When didn't it?

'Almost too late as usual, Mike,' she declared harshly. 'Angry-fist was on the brink of claiming these folks' scalps.'

Their eyes met and Covington sighed.

'Miss Goodnight! I don't know what you think you're doing here, but wouldn't you be better off someplace else? I've just saved these folks' lives and I suggest shadowing reservation jumpers is a game too hot for a scallywag to play.'

Lil's hackles rose. 'Never has been in the past!'

'Hold hard!' Abner put in. He'd stood back and his long brown fingers had been nimbly filling a wheatstraw paper with tobacco from a Bull Durham sack. The building of his smoke was stilled.

'We're in Misfit Lil's debt, soldier

boy. She fired the first warning shots an' she fixed a redskin who got awful near our nags.'

Covington pulled the glove off his right hand and slapped it against his left palm. Lil recognized the gesture for what it was — an attempt to keep a leash on his inclination to anger.

'If I may say so,' he said supercil-iously, 'such — *escapades* aren't a fitting pursuit for a respectable young woman. The chore should have been left for the army.'

Abner said, 'If Injun fighting is what she wants, that's fine with us. Me an' Tom got no quarrel with Lil.'

The stage driver nodded vigorously. 'Sure ain't! She's a good ol' gal.'

Old? Less than twenty years of age, Lil didn't know that she liked that part, but she liked Tom's overall drift.

A woman's voice said tentatively in an unfamiliar accent, 'Please — please don't argue. We're safe now . . . '

Eyes swivelled to the speaker, her intervention entirely unexpected.

Lil more than anyone was intensely curious about the strange person she took to be the Englishwoman, Mrs Fitzcuthbert. In travelling cloak and hat, and moreover closely veiled, she was no less a mystery than before. Possibly more. But the creamy whiteness of the small portion of her throat that was visible, and her cultured tones, convinced Lil she was very young and quite lovely.

She was appalled when with a swift, economical gesture, the top-hatted man she took to be Major Fitzcuthbert gave the intriguing creature's behind a smart whack with his odd cane.

'Be quiet, my dear! You speak out of turn, by Jove!'

It gladdened Lil when the apparent Mrs Fitzcuthbert, despite making a small jump when the cane landed, was woman enough to disregard the reprimand.

'But it cannot be passed over that the girl in the strange clothes also saved our lives, Husband. We saw her shoot down the savage who was about to attack the coach horses. I'm not so unworldly that I cannot appreciate our fate would have been dire if — '

'Silence, woman!' the major roared. 'These are men's matters — *soldiers'* matters. It's out of place for you to take this bizarre apparition's part. I'm sure the lieutenant knows best.'

Covington preened himself and Lil wondered what the hell the Englishman meant by bizarre apparition. Did men's buckskin duds make her that where he came from? Well, maybe they did . . .

'I hope I do, sir,' Covington said. 'Miss Goodnight is unworthy of your wife's kindness. She has a reputation in these parts for her — uh — volatility and impulsiveness. She's quite without charm or manners.'

Fitzcuthbert gave Lil a searching look and his lip curled.

'Indeed . . . Well, Cecilia will not be associating much with the local citizenry, least of all known miscreants. We're from England, you know.'

'I figured you were, sir,' Covington said.

Lil was seldom at a loss for a quick retort, but she didn't know quite what to make of this foreign gent, or how she should respond to someone who was a visitor in her country.

Nor did she want to store up trouble for Liam O'Grady by alienating him. She had happy memories of when the man who was now her troubled boss had been just a fool kid, a happy-go-lucky idiot, a-chasing cows and getting into scrapes that didn't signify . . .

She confined herself to a dismissive 'Huh!'

Covington cleared his throat, clearly relieved by her failure to give Major Fitzcuthbert the comprehensive sass he knew she was capable of.

'My men will help lift the coach back on the roadway and provide an escort to Silver Vein. I suggest you avail yourself of the same protection, Miss Goodnight.'

'Thanks, Mike, but no thanks. I'm a

working girl now — ' She broke off, realizing how the description she'd given herself was commonly used.

Covington — judging by the blush that came to his handsome, clean-shaven face — did, too.

Lil took delight in his discomfiture before a senior ex-military man he was obviously keen to impress. She touched her heels to Rebel to ride around them, scarcely stifling laughter.

But as she set course for High Meadows she knew she hadn't seen the last of the English visitors. A gut feeling told her their paths would cross and recross . . . and the encounters wouldn't be happy.

# 6

## Dirty Work and Play

In the event, the trail of what Misfit Lil and others later came to refer to as the Black Dog disaster took several other twists before Lil next came into contact with the Fitzcuthberts.

Life at High Meadows proceeded at what Lil presumed had become the accustomed, lackadaisical pace. As with the matter of the sleepers, few of the normal chores were done thoroughly. The little work completed adequately was carried out by Liam O'Grady, Lil herself, or with bad grace by the slovenly crew.

Small wonder the outfit was showing no profits!

Liam made several trips to Silver Vein, but Major Fitzcuthbert did not show up to make any prompt, on-the-spot inspections. Liam reported that the major had found 'other business' to preoccupy him in town. Lil didn't ask whether he'd seen the Englishman's wife, but she did ascertain the Fitzcuthberts were renting one of the best houses in town, made vacant by the shooting death in Green River of Flash Sam Whittaker, who'd run a now-defunct gambling hall in whose collapse she and Jackson Farraday had played a stirring part.

If Lil had expected to experience at High Meadows a return to the good times she'd known at the Flying G in her childhood, she was disappointed. Her pa's ranch had been a square outfit where good-natured banter, comradeship, duty and loyalty to the brand had set a happy tone. Though the Flying G cowpokes had been rough-spoken, ready-fighting men of the saddle and rope, they'd subscribed to doing a month's work for a month's wages and to fair play. Here, avoidance, selfishness and smartness were the order of every day.

And Lil suspected deeper deviousness was afoot that she hadn't yet been able to fathom.

Soon after her arrival, Lil noticed that Mary O'Grady was spending far more time away from the High Meadows ranch house than might be expected of a rancher's wife. The absences had occurred several days in a row. Once, she'd not made it to the supper table.

Lil had never been a girl who would hold her tongue out of some misguided notion that it would be rude to question her employer and host. She voiced her puzzlement.

'Where does your beautiful wife take herself off to, Liam? What's up? Is it safe for her to go out riding on her lonesome so regular? I could go along . . . that is, if you'd both like.'

Liam was disconcerted. Lil knew of old that his dark eyes could be as quick to show anger as his lips could be to break into a smile. But this was something different. Liam's face was sober and weary — and shadowed by a strange, frowning uncertainty.

'Mary has a job she goes to in Black Dog,' he said, looking more shamefaced than ever.

Lil's eyebrows arched in surprise. 'A job in Black Dog! But her place is here, and there's plenty that needs her womanly touch at High Meadows.'

'Times are hard, Lil,' he growled. 'We can't make HM pay. Our earnings are percentage- and performance-based. Diminishing returns mean less money for Mary and me as well as our absentee bosses.'

A worrying thought came abruptly to Lil.

'Hell, what kind of work is there for Mary in Black Dog?'

'She cleans. At that new hotel they've thrown up — the Great Western, they call it.'

Lil knew about the pretentiously named hotel. It was the biggest building in the fast-growing mining settlement, built with lumber and by carpenters brought in at no small expense from Silver Vein. No one seemed to know who'd financed it, but it was run by a tough old crone called Aggie Ryan. For those who could afford its prices, it was a quasi-saloon as well as a hotel. Lil had wondered whether it was also a quasi-brothel, as such establishments tended to be.

'Hell . . . ' she said again, this time heaving a sigh. It wasn't like Liam to be so low, so down in the dumps. Maybe his defeatism was also clouding his critical eye.

'Black Dog don't so much call for cleaning as cleaning up,' she went on. 'Is it a good idea for Mary to be going there?'

Liam opened his mouth as though to reply, then he closed it and shook his head firmly.

'You're taking an all-fired interest in our affairs, Lil. There's good wages in Black Dog and we need the money. Mary's made as much money cleaning at the Great Western as I've made punching cows all season.' He grunted deep in his throat. 'You can't argue with that.'

It came to Lil with a chill that Liam was denying his own misgivings; that he was aware he was failing in this respect, just as he was failing, by hiring on a ruffian crew, to keep the HM up to scratch.

'Well, it ain't like you, Liam . . . to ask no questions. Black Dog has a reputation as the rowdiest camp for miles around. A blot on the landscape. Gunfights are two a penny; saloons and gambling dens and God knows what else do business 'round the clock.'

With that, Lil left O'Grady alone, staring into the parlour's smouldering log fire, his unsmiling lips tightly compressed, hands clasped, jaw jutting obstinately. Looking darkly thunderous.

★　★　★

Lil was well aware her veiled warning had exacerbated Liam O'Grady's doubts and the suspicions he'd tried to discount. She'd intended nothing less.

Concerned herself, heavy-hearted, she hid away in a dark corner of the barn to wait what long knowledge of the man told her would be O'Grady's reaction. While she waited, she cleaned and oiled her guns, a pair of old Colt revolvers with much-worn wooden handles. Made sure they were correctly loaded. Her familiarity with the task meant she could work almost by touch alone, polishing with a soft rag, checking actions, testing the smoothness of the cylinders.

She couldn't let him go on his own, she told herself.

Ten minutes passed before Liam left the house. Being proved right in her assumptions brought Lil no elation. The range boss wasn't equipped to let personal matters prey on his mind for long. Likely her disturbing reminders about the unsavoury character of Black Dog had robbed him of what little was left of his uneasy calm. As a younger fellow, he'd been inclined to impetuosity.

She watched O'Grady go to the horse corral, where he roped and saddled his most reliable mount, a bay gelding.

She didn't hurry. She knew where he would be riding. Rebel was rested and could quickly make up any lead the bay might gain. It went without saying that Lil meant to be on hand when O'Grady stormed into Black Dog. Too bad if she'd forced events to a crisis. It was exactly the kind of thing Jackson Farraday would disapprove of and Mike Covington would condemn. But hey, could they have done anything better in what she'd recognized instantly as an emergency?

Liam set off at a raking gallop. He spared neither himself nor his horse, but even so Lil wasn't far back when at length he rode at reckless speed between the tents and shacks of Black Dog and into what was developing into a main drag between more permanent structures.

He flung himself from the tiring bay outside the new hotel, loosely wrapping the reins round a hitch rail at the one vacant spot left. The lumber of the rail, the veranda posts and the building itself were still white and new where the task of painting them a garish pink-cum-scarlet had yet to be completed. Lil was in time to see him push past a blocky figure evidently acting as a doorman and enter the place at a purposeful run.

She was alarmed. Although she knew he couldn't hear, she said, 'Whoa, Liam! Hold up, feller! You might be risking your life — Mary's, too — bulling in like that!'

The Great Western was buzzing with music, rough laughter and the shriller voices of women. Some kind of entertainment was in progress. Lil found a place to leave Rebel across the street and hastily flung herself down from the saddle.

A disgruntled doorman, having failed to delay the last arrival, moved to bar her way as she went up the steps to the hotel veranda. 'Charge of two bucks fer the show, mist — '

She never knew whether he was more surprised to find that close-up she was no mister, or to receive a hard boot to the knee that nearly spilled him and left him hopping on his sound leg while clutching the damaged other.

'Jesus . . . What's happenin' 'round here?'

Lil went through the deserted lobby and straight through double doors that opened into the main saloon. Many of the lights, including those of the imposing central chandelier, had been dimmed. Most of the patrons were crowded round a stage at one end where musicians played, one girl sang — or tried to sing — and a line of others of the hostess type danced.

In the poor, smoky light, Lil couldn't make out where Liam O'Grady was.

Bodies all around were jostling to get closer to the stage and dancers. Hands clutching paper money were waved above the heads. When one of the would-be spenders burst through the throng to the stage's edge, he'd hold out his money to one of the girls. Mostly, she obliged by leaning over, confronting him with an eye-boggling *décolletage*, or by turning around, raising skirt and frilly petticoats, and bending over.

The man then stuffed his bill into the cleavage or gartered stocking top conveniently displayed for the purpose. He'd be egged on by cheers and laughter and would make the best of his brief chance to grope.

One donor, impatient to enjoy his prize before the performance was over, actually managed to clamber on to the stage and pulled a girl out of the lineup. She didn't resist as he led her up stairs at the back of the stage and they stumbled on to a darkened balcony. A door, one in a series, briefly showed an oblong of light as it opened and shut in the upper gloom. The pair's flight to privacy prompted bawdy laughter.

'Hey! Ed's taken one of 'em away!'

'Watch him, Suzy — he's got somethin' for yuh an' it rhymes with pick!'

'Real good for openin' tunnels likewise!'

Suddenly, a roar of rage cut through the rumble of lewd witticisms.

'God-a'mighty — *Mary!*'

It was Liam O'Grady. He'd spotted his wife at the same moment as Lil.

Lil's worst fears were confirmed. Mary O'Grady was one of the Great Western's dancing girls!

It was no wonder she hadn't recognized her first-off. Like the other girls, she wore a shiny red satin gown which was held together at the front by criss-crossed white lacing and had a flounced skirt concealing her black-stockinged legs to no lower than the knee . . . not only that far on the higher dance kicks.

Mary's hour-glass figure looked like it had been shoe-horned into the tight-fitting dress. Her neck and shoulders were exposed. Her generous breasts strained at the front and plainly it would take only the appropriate tug of a lace end to cause them to spill free from the low-cut bodice.

Liam began wading madly through the crowd, flinging men aside in his anxiety to rescue his wife from their ogling and their anticipation of possible further favours once the stage numbers ended and less-structured disorderliness took over.

Many of the spectators were burly, weather-hardened prospectors who didn't take kindly to Liam's aggressive interruption of the progress of their pleasure. Fancy, sporting women were among the commodities in Black Dog that were scarce and high-priced. Supply — maybe deliberately on the part of those who exploited the miners — never met the demand. And some were intoxicated by drink as well as alluring female flesh provocatively dressed.

'Take it easy, brother — yuh're spoilin' the party!'

'Goddamnit! Quit shovin'! Only

plenty *dinero*'ll git yuh a piece o' the vixens!'

But Liam was merely further incensed by their objections. He brushed a drinker aside; pushed another back with a hand planted over his silly, smirking face.

'Let me through, you bastards!'

They replied to Liam's hasty, sweeping hands in kind. Punches were thrown. Liam tried to draw a gun, but the edge of a calloused hand smashed across his forearm, numbing it and causing him to drop the gun from suddenly paralysed fingers.

Lil thought, maybe as well, gunfire in this enclosed place would be apt to lead to unjustified deaths.

Mary stopped dancing. Her hand went to her mouth, which was open in horror. The music played on regardless and her companions kept kicking up their heels and throwing up their skirts. But Mary jumped from the stage.

Lil couldn't tell whether her intention was to run away and hide or to go to Liam. Before she'd taken more than a few steps into the audience, she was engulfed in a grabbing mêlée. Her bodice naturally came unlaced, and Lil lost sight of her as she went down under a pile of men fighting to lay hot hands on the uncovered bounty.

Lil had scant time for dismay before she realized Liam, too, was in urgent need of help.

Liam had managed to dodge a second chopping blow aimed at his throat, but more punishing punches were being exchanged, and Lil felt powerless to intervene. A blow smashed Liam's lips into his teeth and his mouth began to bleed.

'Stop it!' Lil yelled. But no one took a jot of notice.

Liam toppled, or was tripped, and the hotel's disgruntled, snarling patrons applied heavy miner's boots to his fallen body. His foolhardy rush against hopeless odds had set him up for a vicious, maybe fatal stomping.

The savage kicking had to be stopped somehow — and fast. Lil drew her

Colts and fired both into the ceiling.

Pointing the smoking Colts menacingly, she said, 'Let him up, you fools! We don't want killings — just to take home his wife!'

The drunks — for that's what most of them were — were mighty testy, but they didn't want to argue with a crazy girl firing off pistols. They backed off.

'Ain't you that deadshot gal they call Misfit Lil?'

'We ain't arguin', missy. Not over a two-bit whore.'

Liam roared again, 'Why, you — !'

'Shut up, Liam,' Lil said urgently. Her gaze swept the dimly lit saloon again, and to her alarm couldn't find the pack she was looking for. 'Mary's been dragged off. We haven't got time for more brawling.'

Lil was sure Mary hadn't been taken away from the saloon, since she, Lil, had been between the stage and the outer doors throughout. The only other visible exits were the doors off the balcony.

At least two of the ringleaders who'd piled on to Mary were also missing.

'They must've taken her upstairs,' Lil rapped.

Liam went bounding up the stairs two at a time. Lil backed after him, holding the subdued, sullen crowd at bay with her guns.

Liam, swaying and breathless, said, 'Where?'

Lil flung open the first door. She gaped.

'Oh damn! What have we here?'

The room was scarce more than a cubicle. In it, a woman Lil could only partly see was engaged very thoroughly by two miners, who pushed her back and forth between them. She was on hands and bended knees on the tapestry-covered, padded top of an incongruously exotic ottoman. Her red satin dancing outfit had been unlaced and discarded in a crumpled heap on the floor.

The occupants and scant furnishings filled the dimly lit, cell-like place wall to wall. The woman's broad-hipped torso was a rigid curve, supported by braced arms and black-stockinged legs at shoulder and thigh.

When Lil opened the door, she tried to say something, but her mouth was too full to make words. 'Mmmn! Mmmnhh!' was all she could manage to squeeze past. Then she was shuddering all over.

Whether it was in fear, anger or other reaction, Lil was unable immediately to figure.

# 7

## The Shooting Upstairs

When the woman's wide, swivelling
eyes alerted him, the man holding her
face between his hands turned and
bellowed at Lil, 'Git out, peeper!'

The other man opened his closed
eyes, snapped shut his gasping mouth
and brought his thrown-back head
level. 'What the hell . . . ?'

The woman on all fours pulled loose.
Lil saw thankfully that though the red
outfit on the bare floorboards was
almost identical to the costume worn
by Mary O'Grady, the woman getting
up from the cushion-topped box wasn't
her. Nor were the men from among
those who'd fallen on Liam's wife when
she'd left the stage.

The woman, a typical 'upstairs girl',
had bleached hair piled on top of her

101

head and a fake beauty spot over her right cheekbone. She wiped a hand over her lips and said, 'Yeah, what the hell? Run along, freak!'

Lil poked out her tongue and went.

Liam was at the next door. He hurled it open. And from inside, Mary screamed.

His gun lost in the fracas downstairs, Liam yelled to Lil, 'Kill the bastards!'

But Lil couldn't see much past him beyond a confused impression of partly clothed bodies.

'For hell's sakes, mister, what's your game?' a man demanded. He was one of three in a room that was bigger and less spartan than its neighbour and was furnished with a double bed.

'That's my wife you've snatched!' Liam exploded. 'A clean-living, married woman! Set her loose!'

One of the men was sprawled atop of Mary on the bed. He sniggered.

'It's no nevermind what yuh says the damned bitch is, mister. They poke no diff'rent. 'Sides, she's taken money — it spilled outa her bodice, see? That's good as she's gave consent. She stays right here till we've had what's owed. Wanna watch?'

Confident he had the whip hand, he went to pull a knife from a sheath at the back of his belt. 'I'll let my Bowie kiss her breast an' she'll show how willin' she is to wriggle outa her drawers.'

Liam rushed him. 'Get your paws offa her!'

It did him no good.

The third man tripped him and bashed him brutally on the side of the head. He went down with a crash.

The first man said, 'Whatever yuh think she was, cow-nurse, she's gonna be a proper soiled dove afore yuh gits her back!'

'No way!' Lil snapped. 'And I've two loaded guns that says it!'

The third man chimed in scornfully, 'Huh! There's one of you heeled but three of us. I say that means we get to call the tune.'

He had a holstered revolver, a Smith

& Wesson Schofield, and went to draw it.

That was his mistake. Lil was known to all in the district but Black Dog's Johnny-come-latelys as the Princess of Pistoleers. She didn't mess around. She promptly shot him and he stumbled, seriously wounded in the chest, over Liam who was lying dazed. He sank, moaning and bleeding, to the raw, unpolished floorboards.

'The bitch shot me!' he said.

'You tipped your hand with your blather,' Lil informed him coldly. 'Now we're quitting and the lady comes with us.'

With the reek of gunsmoke and blood in the room, no one seemed anxious to argue the point. The man reaching for his Bowie thought better of it; thoughts different from rape paralysed the other. Nor did it seem the patrons remaining downstairs were inclined to investigate. Once lead was whizzing, it was wiser to be doing your carousing someplace else.

Mary pushed free from her frozen tormentor and the bed. She scrambled off the crumpled, stained covers, clutching her opened bodice and trying to relace it.

'Omigod! I didn't want you to know!'

'That's spilt milk,' Lil said tersely. 'Let's get you and Liam out of this hell-hole.'

The man kneeling on the bed said, 'Christ, Jethro's *dying*.'

Liam was groggy but got to his feet. 'You've shot a man, Lil. What do we do?'

'Run for it, of course!'

They suited action to words. The saloon below was half-empty. A man they met at the foot of the stairs backed off.

'I ain't in this,' he bleated. 'I ain't gonna give no trouble!'

The trio rushed outside to their two waiting horses. They'd no time to fetch Mary's mount, wherever it was stabled, and she climbed up behind her husband. The bay lurched into a canter.

Lil made a running leap into the saddle of Rebel.

As they rode off, late, half-hearted calls were raised to stop them. Lil blasted a couple of wild shots in the direction of the shouting.

It was growing full dark and Lil, though a fine markswoman, was on horseback, moving away at speed. Her lead hit only the hotel's frontage, chewing splinters from a scarlet veranda railing, smashing the valuable glass of a window, and raising a last chorus of angry, cheated cries.

★　★　★

Lilian Goodnight was unusually embarrassed. Though she dared not tell Mary, she thought the woman had been a goddamned fool, acting quite out of character and possibly breaking her husband's heart.

Though Mary's junior, she was blunt when they were safely back in the ranch house at High Meadows. She thought the time had come to be blunt.

'What was it all about, Mary? How can you expect Liam ever to forgive you?'

Mary shook her head. 'I beg of you both not to condemn me. I know it seems wrong and horrific now, but what Aggie Ryan asked of me didn't seem so outrageous, so wrong . . . just to dress up and dance and maybe sing instead of swamp out dirtied rooms.'

Lil laughed hollowly. 'If I hadn't needed to help you and Liam get away, I would have gone through that blasted hotel shooting it up in all directions. It was plainly a brothel and a nasty one at that. Why did you agree to do what Aggie Ryan wanted?'

A furtive hint of apology came into Mary's eyes.

'For the money, of course, Lil. Why else does any woman get herself into a situation like that?'

'Well, I ain't easy to shock, but I was.' She took in the utter lifelessness that seemed to have taken hold of the woman's husband. 'Surely it wasn't fair on Liam either.'

'Liam had a hand in it, and he knows it! That's why he's gone so quiet — not just because he was battered about, kicked and hit on the head.'

Lil frowned in puzzlement. 'I'm sorry. You'll have to explain. I'm sure Liam has been an honourable husband. He always behaved honourable when I was not much more'n a button and knew him at my father's Flying G. So do tell.'

Liam made a weak protest, his eyes stony. 'Stop it, Lil! We don't want to tell. It'll only lead to more upset.'

But Lil, a past master at aggravation and never one to feel guilty about it, was insistent.

'I won't stay here and stand by you less'n I'm told!'

Liam gave only an odd, choked cry, but Mary, white-faced and shaking not only from delayed reaction to the day's experiences, began a faltering account.

'Lil, Lil . . . if only we could turn

back the clock. Yes, Liam was honourable — *is* honourable. But he'd reached that sad point where honourable men must cease to be honourable and think only of saving their own skins. He'd been fiddling the High Meadows books, falsifying accounts. You know why I sought work in Black Dog? Because I was desperate to do something toward putting the deficit right before Major Fitzcuthbert can find it out — expose my husband — ruin him!'

Mary finished on a sob.

Lil knew she hadn't heard it all. 'Don't stall now,' she said, quietly persistent. 'There has to be more to this. Why has Liam been cheating on HM's owners?'

'Listen, Lil,' Liam said tonelessly, 'it's plumb crazy for a gal to delve into why men do this or that. It'll do no good now.'

But Mary took a deep breath and answered.

'Liam's always been fond of all kinds of games — you know that. Cards and gambling not excluded. Well, he began visiting the tent saloons that sprang up at Black Dog. The one bet I'd've made was that the games in that wild place were rigged. Marked decks, aces up sleeves and suchlike. He got into the debt of Cullen Fowler, the cattle buyer — a card shark if ever there was one. He borrowed against the ranch's books to try to recoup his losses. Fowler then obliged him to sell him HM stock at knock-down prices or face ruin anyway, by exposure to his employers — perhaps worse: a spell in the penitentiary.'

Lil felt her spirits sink, but much suddenly became clear to her and she wasn't overwhelmingly surprised. She also realized there was still more she had to know.

'How does this tie in with the damnfool way High Meadows is being run? A crew of incompetents and bad-hats can only compound the ranch's losses.'

Again it was Mary who gave the answer.

'They're on the payroll on Fowler's recommendation — on his say-so in truth. Fowler is slick and clever. The ground's being prepared, you see. It needs only Fowler's word when the time is ripe and his riff-raff'll make one last, big rustling swoop and clean out HM! Fowler will see to the brand-blotting where necessary and he has contacts established with meat companies that ask no questions. I wanted to right the book losses and give Liam a chance to stand up to Fowler, fire the hardcase hands he'd planted here, and stop the final blow coming to pass.'

Liam groaned. 'It's no use, Mary. We're obliged to go along with the whole scheme now — share in the spoils and make a new life for ourselves someplace else.'

Lil thought he was deluding himself. 'Do you think Cullen Fowler will let that happen?' she scoffed. 'I reckon when it comes to it he'll claim your cut was used to clear your debts. You won't have any better a leg to stand on than you do now.'

Mary gritted her teeth. 'I'll have to go back to Aggie Ryan — apologize for the ruckus at the Great Western. You must let me make some money, if only enough for us to cut and run.'

'I won't have you working in Black Dog!' Liam said, showing a revived spark of his fire.

'You let me before!'

'But you lied to me! I didn't know you'd be selling your body!'

'Oh, God in heaven — nor did I! I was forced — '

Lil stood up and placed herself between them.

'Quit arguing! No way does Mary go back to Aggie Ryan's. We're all tuckered out after what happened back there. Give a body a chance to *think* . . . '

But Lil feared she'd find no quick answers. Her friends were in a real bad fix.

And in a sudden flash, thinking of Jackson Farraday and what he expected from her, she knew, too, that her loyalties were impossibly divided.

# 8

## The Lost Wife

At first light, after a near sleepless night, Misfit Lil took the dilemma for a walk.

She was torn. She wanted to side with Liam O'Grady, because she shared fond memories with him of the old days at the Flying G. She'd realized post-adolescence that he'd been a true friend to a lonely and vulnerable tomboy of whom he'd had plenty of chances to take advantage but hadn't.

Moreover, the O'Gradys had lately offered her a home and a life of the kind she favoured when others were willing only to condemn her morals and perpetuate the indecent details of her all-too-recent public humiliation at the Fort Dennis ball.

Finally, the O'Gradys had let her

know — albeit as the result of determined questioning — about the ghastly mire they'd stumbled into at High Meadows. It would be easier to drag a cow out of a bog than to rescue them, especially since Liam now seemed set on going all the way to bad. Liam was ready to wipe out the investment of people who'd given him their trust — if only to stop his plucky Mary from offering herself up to God knew what in Black Dog . . .

Lil chose a trail through cottonwoods and cedar and reached a shallow stream. Here was gravelly footing and hardpan with a profusion of dark-grey granite boulders, splotched by the orange of ancient lichen. She took off her boots and waded through the cool, clear water, trying to think of something to hum to cheer herself up, but the only music and words that would come to mind were a mockery . . . a pious fraud. It was the refrain to a hymn they'd sung at the academy for young ladies in Boston:

*Peace, peace to my soul*
*Flows like a beautiful river;*
*Peace, hallowed and pure,*
*Constant abiding forever . . .*

She felt all choked up. Peace was the last thing she had.

How could she turn against the O'Gradys and betray their trust?

But how could she not and stay honest?

She thought briefly of the British cattle company agent she'd helped save from Angry-fist's bloodthirsty rebels. He was the representative of the poor devils across the ocean who'd put money into High Meadows and were going to lose it. Could she clear her conscience by telling Albert Fitzcuthbert all she knew?

Intuition told her no. The ex-major had taken an instant dislike to her and she to him. She suspected, for instance, he was a bully and a tyrant to his mysteriously young and veiled wife, Cecilia.

She also thought of the county law in the form of Sheriff Hamish Howard and his toady deputy, Sly Connor. But given the hostile part they'd played in the affair of Corporal Thomas and Fanny Kennedy . . . no, definitely not. They were truly ignorant of the scene and effective at little other than exacting tribute from the citizenry for self-aggrandizement. The O'Gradys were best left free of their hamfisted attentions.

At last, she came to figuring the one point she kept avoiding — that she'd hired on at High Meadows at the instigation of Jackson Farraday, who'd known from the outset something was wrong at the ranch and was expecting her to report back to him.

But she also remembered making the proviso to Jackson that she didn't want to make trouble for Liam. It was tempting for her to do anything that would put herself in Jackson's good books, make him consider her in a generous light where he might give her attention and — dare she imagine it? — his love.

She examined her motives closely. Would telling on the O'Gradys to Jackson amount to ratting for personal reasons, or would it be a better way than any to fulfil her obligations to honesty and justice?

She stopped paddling and sat on a bankside boulder to let her feet dry in the rising sun and mull it over while the stream kept up a careless chuckle . . .

The upshot was that when she returned to the ranch house, she pulled a bluff. She told Mary and Liam she wanted to exercise Rebel, but in fact she rode out for Fort Dennis. And Jackson Farraday.

★   ★   ★

She was in sight of the fort within two hours. It sat on the plain like a fat cat dozing in the mid-morning warmth under a limp flag. As she advanced on it, the solid lumber gates in the stockade fence swung open and a column of riders emerged. Jackson and

Lieutenant Michael Covington were foremost among them. They moved into a brisk, business-like canter.

Sure ain't a reception committee for me, Lil told herself.

She rode to meet them, raising a hand in greeting, her heart foolishly skipping a beat.

'You're a pretty good piece of ground from High Meadows, Miss Lilian,' Jackson said.

'Yup. I've ridden here to see you.'

'Do you have news?'

'Sort of,' Lil said, wary of so many other ears.

Covington edged his horse into the closing gap between them.

'Well, that's as maybe, but Mr Farraday is a busy man and hasn't a moment today for idle gossip with admirers. His tracking skills are in demand.'

His high-handed, officious interruption annoyed Lil.

'You're not ever gonna change are you, Mike Covington? Supposing there's something I need to discuss with Jackson?'

She would have gone on to say he was an ignorant, insufferable stuffed-shirt, but Jackson said warningly, 'Now then, Lil . . . Maybe you can speak with me some other time. The lieutenant is right that we're off on urgent business. So excuse us if you will. It's a risky, delicate matter and every moment might count.'

Lil pursed her lips. Jackson was not prone to exaggeration. Damn it, she thought. 'What's happened?' she asked.

'Major Fitzcuthbert, agent of High Meadows's owners, has reported his wife missing from their house in Silver Vein — presumed kidnapped.'

'Oh, my God! Who would've done that?'

Jackson shook his head doubtfully. 'Fitzcuthbert reckons it's the renegades from the reservation. Their attack on the stagecoach failed, he says, so they're figuring on holding Mrs Fitzcuthbert for ransom.'

'But that ain't Angry-fist's kind of crime,' Lil said promptly.

'Come on, Mr Farraday!' Covington said. 'This is no time for briefing busybodies.'

Lil ignored him and appealed to Jackson. 'Oh, can't you let the impatient lieutenant go ahead for a moment or two?'

The request made Covington colder than ever.

'May I remind you, Miss Goodnight, that I am Mr Farraday's superior here?'

'In what sense?' Lil asked acidly.

Jackson touched his hat brim. 'My apologies, Miss Lilian, but my contract is with the army and I have to defer to the lieutenant. Some other time,' and he rode off to regain his place at the head of the passing detachment.

With what must have been a mighty effort of will, Covington paid no more regard to his exchange with Lil, but swerved to follow Jackson. Oh boy, wasn't he mad!

Deep down, Lil knew that Jackson

would be aware that if the charismatic Apache hothead had indeed grabbed a white woman, he would have planned it well and had an escape route worked out. His bunch would have been unlikely to leave any worthwhile tracks to follow. The Indians were masters at disappearing into the canyonlands; could out-coyote the canniest soldiers or lawmen.

She gazed after the departing troopers, a disgusted, almost sick look on her face. While Mike Covington had Jackson running around on a fool's errand, she needed him! Plainly, her reluctance to speak up in company had been interpreted by Jackson as meaning it was of less than life-or-death importance, and maybe that was true. Whatever . . . she was niggled by the sight of Jackson's tall, straight back turned on her. Worry? Why did she let herself worry? Crazy!

Naturally, her thoughts turned to retaliation, particularly against Covington who, she knew from old, would insist on Jackson following all sorts of false trails and go against best advice till he'd exhausted every improbability.

What if she were to find the missing Cecilia Fitzcuthbert before them? Jackson would take notice then! Not even Mike Covington would be able to brush her off her reasonable request for a confidential moment of his scout's attention.

The soldiers were heading for Angryfist's high-desert haunts to cast around for the tracks of a band of kidnappers. Lil had a hunch the whole story smelled to high heaven. Her brain was working fast. It could be there was another explanation for the Englishwoman's disappearance . . .

She remembered how Major Fitzcuthbert had struck her with his swagger-cane. Granted, it hadn't been much more than a tap, but supposing he was one of those brutes who beat their wives? The cane had looked quite capable of being a fiendish instrument of corporal punishment. It was an interesting chain of 'what if?' and Lil knew what the answer would be if a husband treated her like that. She'd run away at the very least.

It was a line of thought Mike Covington would be too hidebound to pursue. He saw all men who'd attained superior military rank to himself as persons to respect and admire; never to question. In that respect he was so unlike herself that she wondered why Jackson could ever hint that he'd make a good match for her. Sure, he was all handsome and debonair, of the right, marriageable age and with good prospects, but they were alike as chalk and cheese.

Anyway, her thoughts were straying. She wasn't considering her own fortunes, but Cecilia Fitzcuthbert's. It would be easy for her, Lil, to run away from a bullying husband — not that she'd marry one in the first place, though some girls were given no choice — because she knew the country here like the back of her hand and had all the skills to survive. But the young

Englishwoman didn't, and surely hadn't.

Pluck alone wouldn't take Mrs Fitzcuthbert far, Lil reasoned. Therefore, if her wild guess was right, she wasn't going to be found in the mountains or canyons, where Angry-fist could have taken her, but somewhere close to Silver Vein.

Convincing herself she'd hit upon a truth that had evidently escaped Mike Covington and Jackson, Lil turned Rebel's head, kicked at his sides and set off at a smart lope for the vicinity of the township.

The town itself had places where a person could hide, but a stranger would know of only the most obvious, especially if she'd been kept in seclusion, as the British agent had kept his wife. Lil's understanding was that Cecilia had not been allowed to make new friends, in keeping with Fitzcuthbert's promise to Mike Covington that she wouldn't be associating with the locals. Without help, and if Cecilia had been hiding in the hayloft of the livery barn, for instance, she would already have been found.

Lil embarked on a horseback tour of the many places within walking distance of the town where citizens were known to retreat for picnics or private rendezvous.

Time and again, she drew a blank in a prettily wooded basin or at a placid lakeside. She began to wonder whether she was on as big a wild-goose chase as the army party following up Fitzcuthbert's Indian kidnap claim.

Maybe Cecilia Fitzcuthbert was hopelessly lost. Already dead? Murdered?

In flagging spirits — with a growing, quiet desperation — Lil turned to more rugged places to the east and south, once the domain of mountain men and fur trappers and now favoured by the outlaw gangs. It was a naturally confused, fortressed area that led ultimately to deep canyons, rivers and mesas. Hardly the place for a female tenderfoot, Lil observed grimly. Accident or foul play could strike from any quarter.

And so, in the niche of an upland pass, she came to the hidey-hole known by an Indian name that translated to Old Horse Thief's Cave. Its dark entrance in the sandstone was partly obscured by jumbled boulders and a clump of twisted cedars.

The cave was big and dry and said to be haunted by the spirit of a Ute chief who thirtysome years back had assembled a feared band of mounted marauders from several tribes, including the Paiute and his own clan's traditional enemies, the Shoshone. The unlikely bunch had slipped through the mountains to make daring raids on California horse herds, bringing back into Utah more than 2,000 head over the Old Spanish Trail.

There was no knowing what denizens might lurk in this lonely place today. Lil climbed down from her tired horse, hauled out the big .45 on her right hip and advanced warily into the mountain.

Suddenly, a voice cried out tremulously, 'Who's there? Who is it?'

Lil said, 'Well, I ain't no Indian horse thief's ghost. Nor are you!'

# 9

## Cecilia's Story

'They're looking for you all over, Mrs Fitzcuthbert,' Lil told the scared woman. 'In every far-flung place 'cept the right one! What are you doing here?'

'I've run away,' she said. 'You're the girl who saved us from the Indians, aren't you?'

'Yeah, I sorta had something to do with that, ma'am.'

So her surmise was vindicated, Lil thought: Mrs Fitzcuthbert *had* run away. The young Englishwoman, possibly no older than Lil herself, said, 'Don't call me ma'am — you may use my first name, Cecilia. You won't give me away, will you?'

Lil took in Cecilia's parlous condition. Her clothes were torn, muddy and damp, as though she might have fallen into a stream. Her blonde hair was in straggles. She was very pale.

'No, I won't,' Lil said, building a brown-paper smoke. 'I'm Lilian Goodnight. Misfit Lil, some call me on account of an unfair reputation. Another handle they give me is the Princess of Pistoleers. Howsoever, under any name, I'm my own woman and do and tell only as I choose. Want a quirly?' she offered.

Cecilia shuddered involuntarily as she shook her head.

Lil took no slight. She said nonchalantly, 'Run away, huh? How will you cope here, on your lonesome? What will you do for grub? I bet you couldn't catch a rabbit!'

'I brought a carpetbag with me. I packed it with bread, bacon, apples, tea, sugar and some tins. A mug and a small cooking pot, too. Being heavy, the supplies slowed me down considerably.'

Lil struck a lucifer and put its blaze to her rough and ready cigarette. The slack paper crackled loudly as she drew in a lungful of smoke.

'Might've been heavy, but they won't last for ever,' she said, the words coming out in a cloud of smoke.

Cecilia put a hand to her nose and mouth and coughed delicately. 'No, of course not,' she said, downcast.

'But I reckon I could help you,' Lil said encouragingly. Then, bluntly: 'Why'd you run away?'

Cecilia combed her fingers through her hair, trying to tidy it. 'That's a very long story, though I'm quite free of any fault in the matter, I assure you.'

Lil thought she looked very sweet but defensive, like a naughty child who'd gotten herself and her fine clothes mussed up and was concerned that the explanation was going to get her into trouble. Her dirtied hair framed a charming little face and emphasized the delicacy of small, regular features. Lil's previous impression was reinforced — that Cecilia's character was a mysterious, paradoxical affair composed in equal parts of frailty and strength. Tidied up, she would no doubt bloom and look fresh as a daisy. Her clear, bright blue eyes, though red-rimmed just now, suggested honesty.

'I'm willing to listen and believe, and my horse needs resting,' Lil said. 'Fire away.'

The next half-hour was one of explanation and, for Lil, of astonishing revelations. The way of it was sad and tangled.

'Both my mama and papa died in the London Fever Hospital when I was a child,' Cecilia said. 'Fortunately — or perhaps not — I was spared. The physician, Dr Southwood Smith, was influenced by the new French medical science and had insisted on the disinfection and fumigation of our home. Major Albert Fitzcuthbert became my guardian through family connections obscure to me till this day. He was well set-up financially and had certainly had a sound career in the British Army, serving with distinction in India. He was mentioned many times in despatches for his gallantry and had medals, bars and ribbons galore. He took part in the Indian Mutiny campaign of 1857, and was present at the actions of Bhagonalo, Nugeena, Bareilly and Mohunpore. He retired after thirty-three years' service.'

Lil obliquely posed the question that had puzzled her since she'd met the Fitzcuthberts.

'Your husband is much older than you; sixty, I'd say, if he's a day . . . '

For a moment, Lil feared Cecilia might have been on the verge of telling her to mend her manners, but with the heaving of a sigh and her shoulders, she explained.

'Because of his long absences, the major had placed me in a Chelsea boarding-school, where I saw little of the world but what was relatively settled and happy. Then, three years ago, on my sixteenth birthday, he came to the school and withdrew me. He said I was growing out of the school and we must look to my future. He wanted me to be his bride.'

'Well, I knew that I was to come into

an inheritance on my twenty-first birthday that would allow me to live independently in a financial sense, but that was many years away and I had nowhere to go meantime. Also, I knew nothing of love. Misguidedly, I supposed his proposal to be a proper extension of that protection and education I was always told my thoughtful guardian had kindly provided. In my narrow knowledge, the alternative to marriage seemed to be a life in squalor and danger of the kind that had carried off my parents. So I married Fitzcuthbert.'

'And lived to regret it!' Lil said, providing the conclusion most obvious to her.

Shamefacedly, in a small voice, Cecilia said, 'Yes. For three long years he has kept me a virtual prisoner, scarcely allowing me out of his sight.'

'It's the inheritance, of course,' Lil said. 'It has to be. As your husband, he wants to get his hands on your fortune. But that must be sheer greed — a sacrifice of your youth and sweetness to no good purpose, seeing as you said the major has his own money.'

'But he doesn't! Not any longer. It's why he married me, why he works for a salary despite his pension, why we're here in America. Why, in the end, I *had* to run away!'

'Hmm! Fitzcuthbert invested his money foolishly and lost it then,' Lil said.

'Yes — I mean, no. That is, he invested his money at private London gambling clubs. Squandered it, in truth. As a result, he became burdened by personal debt. Further consequences were that household spending descended into frugality and he was perpetually pursued by creditors. He accepted with alacrity the situation of overseer for a syndicate of financiers whose interests are in the Americas. It was both providential and advisable. He came — escaped! — gladly to New York, whence his duties have brought us to Utah. No doubt he counts on a return to England after I've attained my majority and he has received my inheritance.'

Lil laughed inwardly, emptily, suddenly perceiving the dismal joke in the situation. Her friend, Liam O'Grady, had got his tail in a crack due to unwise card-playing, and the man sent to check on him, maybe bring him to book, was a villain of the same but deeper dye.

Ah, but wasn't there an old saying 'set a thief to catch a thief? Here, probably unknown to those who should know, it was a gambler to catch a gambler.

But Cecilia was upset enough and she couldn't say anything like that. What she did say, nodding sympathetically, was, 'A bad business. I know a feller hereabouts that got hooked on gambling. He was trapped by a crooked cattle buyer who can smell a potential victim from miles off better than he can a whole herd of farting longhorns at ten paces. Name of Cullen Fowler — '

Cecilia gasped and went whiter than ever.

'Oh! The very same man!'

'What do you mean?'

'The man who — who . . .'

Lil was exasperated. 'The man who what? You must tell me!'

Eventually, Cecilia was persuaded to tell the last and most harrowing part of her story, which had moved toward its climax in the smoke-filled parlour of the Fitzcuthberts' rented house in Silver Vein . . .

★ ★ ★

Cecilia was filled with consternation. The keyhole in the parlour door permitted her a view across the room within toward the fireplace. In front of it a small table and two chairs had been set for the convenience of her husband and his visitor, Cullen Fowler.

Fowler was one of Albert Fitzcuthbert's newly made 'friends', whom he'd met in the saloons of Silver Vein. He resorted to these places regularly, leaving her in their house to stoke the fire, do the chores, and think she might soon die of boredom. He told her his excursions were in the nature of business, to sniff out the local climate.

Now Cecilia had the evidence that gave foundation to her suspicions. The two men were playing cards and there was hard liquor, a box of big, fat cigars and money on the table. All the money was on Cullen Fowler's side.

Her heart sank as if it had become a heavy stone. As she'd half-guessed, Fitzcuthbert had reverted to his old habit. Once more, he'd been lured into high-stakes games of chance, this time using the only money left to them — the dwindling expenses allowance from his masters in London. Clearly, the association with Fowler had been developed elsewhere and Fitzcuthbert was in neck-deep.

' . . . So fear not, old fellah,' he was saying airily. 'I don't welsh on my debts. Nobody will find out about our little arrangement, and my wife will never dare speak up. Never!'

Cullen Fowler was a big, frightening man who looked like an ape from the jungle got up in broad-cloth store clothes. A scowl lowered his heavy brows.

'Sure, Bertie, I seen her an' she's a pretty little thing — a ripper — but will she be willing?' he asked.

'I'll go fetch her straight away and you shall see that she's properly agreeable and obedient to my wishes.'

Fitzcuthbert rose and not wanting to be exposed as a keyhole-peeper, Cecilia slipped like lightning to the kitchen. The last words she heard were from Fowler.

'Hold hard! Let's fix how we do it first . . . '

After she'd been in the kitchen several minutes and Fitzcuthbert hadn't appeared, Cecilia began to wish she'd stayed and listened. What was it she'd agree to?

Fitzcuthbert duly came to the door and summoned her. In trepidation she went to the parlour. To her surprise, the room was occupied by only her husband. Evidently Cullen Fowler had left. She breathed a little easier as Fitzcuthbert firmly closed the door. The way she'd been obliged to live since her marriage had made her shy with strangers, especially gentlemen she knew only by their acquaintance with Fitzcuthbert.

'I want you to do something for our private betterment, my dear,' he said.

She was puzzled by his manner. It seemed as if he was assuming a playful tone.

'What is it?' she asked.

'A pleasure — a surprise. But I shall need to blind-fold you for maximum enjoyment.'

Her relief at seeing Cullen Fowler gone and the faint hope that he was paying her some small loving attention, if only through a sense of guilt at his evening's gambling and negligence, dispelled her caution and she agreed. Committed by matrimony, a proper Victorian wife had little choice. The husband was the lawful master. Suffer and be still was the expectation; it was implied in a girl's education that the rule was that the female must yield to male aggression.

She let him cover her eyes with a folded silk cravat, which he knotted securely, and wasn't overly surprised when he told her to lean over a sofa and hold its back. It was as she thought. Despite their disparity in age, he was not unaccustomed to demanding his conjugal rights on occasion, nor she in granting them, though she'd never experienced the perfect bliss he'd promised would one day visit her. She could believe the best-qualified medical men of the day who submitted that desire in the well-bred woman was small.

Hands lifted up her petticoats from behind and folded them over her back. Abruptly, her drawers were pulled down and dropped to her ankles, making her shiver. It was exactly as she'd expected, though she didn't think being blindfolded was going to make her appreciate it more. Any attempt to oppose his wishes would be utterly useless, of course.

He told her to maintain the posture of bending over forward, and to free her feet and place them well apart.

Pray let this be over quickly, she thought, feeling like a victim of sacrifice. Tense moments crawled past. She felt hairy legs brush between the soft, inner skin of her own.

'Hold absolutely firm! Hollow your back!' Fitzcuthbert said, and to her immense shock she realized his instructions were coming from another part of the room — even as she was entered from behind.

It was very severe on her. The sensation was worsened by the ordered splaying of her legs and the tight, two-handed grip on her buttocks which the person behind, who could not be her husband, had taken up.

With a horrified shriek, she pulled free from the tight conjunction, hurting herself and precipitating a furious curse from her unknown partner. She tore off the blindfold.

As she should have guessed, the beast in cahoots with Fitzcuthbert in her assault was Cullen Fowler. Beyond him, disturbed curtains at the bay window showed where he'd been hiding when she'd entered the room and unsuspectingly deferred to Fitzcuthbert's seemingly legitimate requests.

'Oh, God!' she exclaimed. 'I faint. I shall die! This isn't right . . . just isn't right!'

'Now, my dear, don't be a noodle!' Fitzcuthbert said. 'The thing was nine-parts done and its completion would have suffered you no real harm. I shall insist you acquiesce later without reserve!'

Cecilia wailed in anguish. '*Why . . . ? In what?*'

It was left to Fowler, licking his lips, to tell.

'It's like this, li'l beauty. All your husband's debts will be discharged by allowing me to spend a night with yourself, doing as I please. I'll teach you how to enjoy it. Hell, it ain't a bad deal at all.'

Cecilia was speechless as an enormous humiliation and disgust fused together. 'Oh . . . '

She curled up at bay on the couch, pulling her skirt down over her feet, and began weeping softly as though her heart would break.

Fowler chuckled. Buttoning pants and tucking shirt-tails into his waistband, he was insensitive to her distress.

'Anyhow, we can complete this later an' continue on the same basis for as long as you're visiting with us in this land of liberty. In the West, virtue ain't set on a damnfool pedestal an' the giving of pleasure is open an' honest. Han'some woman like you shouldn't have to settle for what she gets from an old-timer. Your Bertie an' me can have more fun at the card table — long as he guarantees your surrender.'

'Which I have,' Fitzcuthbert interjected firmly.

'The arrangement is another night to cover ev'ry ten more dollars he bets an' loses. His marital privileges against my dollars. He might win back his money. Contrariwise, my winnings won't cost him another cent. It'll be squared by delicious pokings into your cabinet of love. Ain't that just fine an' dandy for everyone?'

Cecilia had heard enough. She leaped up.

'No, of course it isn't!' she cried. 'It's — it's an earthly hell!'

She rushed from the room and her tormentors. She stumbled upstairs and into her bed where she pulled the covers over her head.

It was not enough to prevent her hearing Fitzcuthbert's confident assurances as Cullen Fowler departed.

'Have no fear, Mr Fowler . . . I'll see it arranged. Mrs Fitzcuthbert shall be — uh — corrected and properly instructed. She'll not dare to oppose my will. If by some absurdity she fails to come to her senses at the double, there'll be stripes on her arse when you next see it, by Jove!'

Fowler stomped down the walk, words thick in his throat.

'I hope so, Bertie. I'd admire to see that ass again real soon. I do declare your wife's right purty from every angle an' our bargain suited me fine.'

Fitzcuthbert called after him, 'She'll be available and compliant I assure you, sir! She'll refuse you nothing, allow full possession . . .'

But in the dubious sanctuary of her bed Cecilia, devastated by what they'd done to her, vowed she wouldn't stay to be violated again.

# 10

## Under Suspicion

Misfit Lil was appalled by Cecilia's story. 'That's terrible! You did right to run away. Matrimony ain't slavery and it ain't for the purpose of making a woman into a whore. You're better free of the major's hobbles.'

Cecilia wasn't easily comforted. By the time she'd told her story, she was scarlet and horribly ashamed.

'Perhaps running away is a sin, too. Major Fitzcuthbert says St Paul tells us in the Scriptures, 'Be subject to the husband as you are to the Lord. For the husband is the head for the wife just as Christ is the head of the Church.' And he repeats it three times, saying at the end 'show reverence to your husband'.'

'I've no time for Bible quoting,' Lil responded. 'Folks make it say anything they want. Howsomever, I also seem to remember it says 'thou shalt not commit adultery' and 'thou shalt not covet thy neighbour's wife', which would be good lessons for Fitzcuthbert and Fowler!'

As a total stranger, confined to a rented house in Silver Vein, it was a marvel Cecilia had stumbled across the cave at all. When questioned, she said, 'I determined to break out of my prison and put my life at the mercy of God in the wilderness.'

'The cave's too close to town to be in what I'd call wilderness,' Lil said. 'But that makes it safer, considering they're searching for you in more distant and rugged parts.' She tutted. 'Your husband misled 'em. Mike Covington — the lieutenant from Fort Dennis, but you wouldn't know *him* — has taken the scout Jackson Farraday to all the wrong places. Why the Army hires experts then lets a fool lieutenant order the job done his way, I can't figure.'

'But I do know Mr Covington. He

was the handsome officer who led the men who helped save us when the Indians chased the stagecoach. He said you were unworthy of my kindness . . . '

'Like I said, he's a fool and you *don't* know him!' Lil insisted. 'But his stupidity will help us keep you hidden. You can stay here and I'll visit you regular; bring supplies and advice and so forth.'

'Oh, Lil! I don't know how long I can hold out on my own. Before you came I was wishing I was dead. I wished it with all my heart. There seems to be no end to the nightmare I live!'

Lil said, 'I liked the spirit you showed in running away better than what you're telling me now. We gals have to stick together. I'll find the answers, I know I will.'

But Lil was less confident than she was pretending to her depressed new friend. Cecilia, she recognized, was more fragile than herself. She didn't have the survival skills for a prolonged sojourn away from civilization. The problems were piling up.

How could she secure the future of a runaway wife and restore the wife's prospect of happiness through an inheritance rightfully hers?

How could she destroy the evil of the crooked gambler and cattle-buyer Cullen Fowler; of the bullying husband and liar Albert Fitzcuthbert?

How could she save High Meadows and the mired O'Gradys from a disastrous rustling plot?

This time, it seemed, Misfit Lil was way out of her depth.

★  ★  ★

Several days later, all parties in the affair seemed to have reached an impasse. The military hadn't found Cecilia Fitzcuthbert. Her husband, it seemed, dithered in Silver Vein. Cullen Fowler was lying low. Cecilia was sinking into depression at the Old Horse Thief's Cave, though Lil had managed to bring her some modest comforts, including candles and well-worn copies of two Waverley novels, *The Pirate* and *Redgauntlet*, which she'd borrowed from Mary O'Grady.

Then Albert Fitzcuthbert arrived at High Meadows. He came unexpectedly in a buggy rented from the Silver Vein livery. The mare's hoofs thudded to a stop in the stomped dirt of the ranch-house yard, and Fitzcuthbert, who was pot-bellied, climbed down ponderously.

'Hullo,' Lil said to Liam O'Grady. 'Is this the new boss come to take over?'

She intended the words to be overheard by the ex-major and the sarcasm wasn't missed.

Clenching his swagger-cane in both hands, he said in a cold fury, 'Curb your tongue, young woman, or I'll see you thrashed and dismissed for insolence! It's none of your business why I'm here. You, sir' — turning to Liam — 'will take me into the house and to whatever serves as your office.'

'Sure, Major,' Liam said, nodding

politely but paling. 'Run along, Lil . . . I may be a considerable time.'

Lil did no running along. She wasted no time in positioning herself under an open window where she could listen in on their conversation. She didn't have to speculate for long on what had precipitated the British agent's visit.

'You've gotten this all wrong, Major,' Liam was saying as they came into hearing. 'There've been no big losses, though I admit the sales made have been at no great profit. It's the prices, you know.'

'No, I don't know!' Fitzcuthbert snapped. 'Nor can I stay in Utah for ever, despite the unfortunate disappearance of my wife. Expenses have — uh — run out and London has wired me urgently. My principals say 'Find out what is happening at High Meadows and advise immediately.''

Liam said heavily, 'Last winter was bad — snow, icy winds and sub-zero temperatures took a high toll of cattle stranded on the ranges. A series of storms was no help.'

'Reports reaching England don't show it was much worse than is normal,' Fitzcuthbert said scathingly. 'By Jove, it's your job to *manage*! That doesn't mean allow the herds to drift aimlessly with no food or water — to huddle and die in masses.'

'They didn't.'

'Then you should have no problem.'

Lil wanted to leap up and shout the truth: Liam has a no-good crew forced on him by your dirty new friend, Cullen Fowler. How can he make a go of it with a bunkhouse stacked against him?

'But see here,' Fitzcuthbert said, riffling through pages. 'I'm sure the prices for stock sold are far below market averages. Something is up! I'll make further enquiries. If you're a cheat and a thief, as the sums suggest, I may have to put the evidence to the board and call in the law. For now, I insist on taking these tally books with me, Mr O'Grady. They'll be checked independently and most thoroughly.'

The injustice of it had Lil seething and by the time Fitzcuthbert was leaving, she could hold in her indignation no longer.

She stepped into Fitzcuthbert's path as he strode from the house, carrying the possibly incriminating records.

'A word with you, Major Fitzcuthbert!'

'You!' Fitzcuthbert said, startled out of his engagement in mean and vengeful thoughts. 'Out of my way, young woman! I've been told about you, and I assure you I've absolutely nothing I would wish to discuss with a person of your class!'

He waved the swagger-cane at her.

Lil was forced to step back to avoid being struck.

'Hey! What right've you got to raise a stick at me? There's plenty we gotta discuss — like your pal Cullen Fowler, f'r'instance. He's a bigger trickster and crook than Liam O'Grady, and I happen to know you're in his clutches.'

'What's that you say?' His voice rose

high, ending in a squawk. 'Rubbish! Stand aside, I say! I'll not listen to tall stories from a gossip!'

'I'm no gossip, but there's no denying you're a vicious bully and a liar!'

Fitzcuthbert gave an inarticulate roar of rage, and said, 'I take strong exception to that remark! You're a troublemaker and a dirty young trollop to boot, I understand. You've been warned. Get out of the way, or you'll be disfigured by a cut of the cane!'

Thus he forced his way to the buggy. He bounded to the seat, swapped his cane for the whip from the bracket, and put the mare into more rapid motion than was her custom.

Lil was left in the cloud of the buggy's dust, hands on hips, staring after him.

Liam came up behind her.

'You shouldn't have antagonized him, Lil. We don't want him finding reasons for giving us extra attention. Just remember who he is. It won't hurt to give him respect. It ain't helpful to make wild accusations without foundation.'

Lil hadn't told Liam about sheltering Cecilia and what she'd learned from her.

'Well, he's got — a certain stink about him,' she suggested. 'That's the foundation.'

'Nope. That's just some pomade he was wearing, Lil.'

'You'll see,' Lil muttered. 'He's a bad 'un, I swear.'

She made herself scarce and Liam seemed happy to let her go. He had his problems to mull on . . .

But Lil didn't intend to let it rest. She was still raring to confront Albert Fitzcuthbert with his crimes. She knew a powerful lot. If she used her knowledge to best advantage, she figured she might get Liam and Mary off the hook. High Meadows could also be saved yet.

★ ★ ★

Lil saddled up Rebel and rode out for Silver Vein. Using cross-country side-trails, she was confident she could reach the township ahead of Fitzcuthbert.

The best place to corner him would be behind the closed doors of his own rented house. Catching him unawares, and without witnesses, she could force him to listen to her. Once he realized she knew so much about his misconduct, and if she threatened to report it to his masters in England, the rest ought to be simple. He'd be none the wiser if she hinted she had a friendly telegraph clerk to help her in return for past 'favours'. He'd be sure to swallow that. After all, blasted Mike Covington had convinced him she was a bad girl.

He'd call it blackmail, and it would be. It was a damned dirty way of doing it, but to Lil's mind it was justified. An *honest* blackmail, she reassured herself.

The last few miles to Silver Vein were covered in short order. Lil slipped from the saddle and tethered Rebel behind some cottonwood-shaded houses 300 yards away from the large frame house that had once belonged to Flash Sam Whittaker.

In Lil's opinion, it was a most pretentious dwelling for the small town, being papered and carpeted. The room she broke into after five minutes' struggling with a rusty window catch was unused. She crouched behind the ghostly shapes of dustcloth-draped furniture, and checked a gun.

From here on, it was going to be easy as falling off a horse drunk.

★  ★  ★

Cullen Fowler had been keeping half an eye on the residence occupied by the Fitzcuthberts. His impatience with the agent of the British cattle company was growing. Cheating was deeply ingrained in him as a primary course of action. Consequently, it was also in his nature to suspect everyone else of the same.

The story of Fitzcuthbert's kidnapped wife hadn't gone down well with him. Savvy folks were saying it didn't ring true. To himself, with his secret knowledge, it rang even less true.

It was possible Fitzcuthbert had broken their bargain and had himself spirited away his delectable wife to deny him payment of the agreed favours in settlement of the gambling debts. But it was impossible for him, Cullen Fowler, to come out and air his suspicions publicly in Silver Vein without divulging his less-than-innocent role in the matter, thereby jeopardizing the respect of clean-thinking cattlemen . . . let alone the confidence of those he might try to cheat.

No way would speaking up be good for his business, in cattle or with cards.

Frustrated, Fowler kept a watch on Fitzcuthbert's movements. When an informant from the livery, in exchange for a cheap bottle of rotgut, told him Fitzcuthbert had finally ventured to visit High Meadows, he awaited the dupe's return with interest, taking a window seat in McHendry's saloon, sipping whiskey thoughtfully and denying himself poker-playing profits.

Would Fitzcuthbert return accompanied by Cecilia?

Not that Fowler suspected the frightened wife had been clandestinely boarded with the O'Gradys. That didn't fit with the personalities and facts of the case as he knew them.

What Fowler saw in due course was the hurried arrival of Misfit Lil and her furtive disappearance behind the rear of the unoccupied house.

This unexpected development exercised his devious brain frantically. He'd understood from his planted men that Lilian Goodnight, a well-known scallywag, was riding for High Meadows — making minor trouble there in truth, throwing her weight around in excess of its actuality, nobbling bulky Red Ballinger by sheer happenstance on day one, and raising embarrassing questions about unbranded cows.

How the devil was she involved?

Twisting an empty glass in a big hand, Fowler decided that by one means or another he was going to get the answer.

# 11

## Wild American Girl

Misfit Lil waited inside the house without moving as the minutes passed. It was late afternoon and darkness in the closed room steadily deepened. Her ears were straining to catch the slightest sound.

Major Fitzcuthbert's arrival was announced by the grate of a key in an unoiled lock. Lil tensed, every nerve and muscle on the alert.

She heard him enter and move around in the house beyond the closed room where she was hiding. Light made a thin outline around the edges of its door as Fitzcuthbert lighted lamps. It was time to show herself.

Fitzcuthbert uttered a soldierly oath when she walked boldly into his parlour.

Jumping up from the table where he'd seated himself with a bottle and a glass, he said, 'What the blue blazes are you doing here? You've broken in! Get out, and leave behind anything you've pinched!'

'I'm not a thief, mister.'

'Get out, I say, or I'll give you a caning and have the law on you!'

But one of Lil's guns leapt into her hand, there so swiftly that Fitzcuthbert's eyes bulged from their sockets.

'Oh dear, that ain't the way to talk to a girl who might've lost her way,' she said coolly.

Fitzcuthbert's laugh was brittle. 'You don't look like a girl who loses her way.'

'Looks can be deceiving, but maybe you're right and I am here a-purpose.'

'If you're looking for business, you can also get out. I don't need a whore!'

'I ain't a whore and I'd never offer myself to you in any case. I wouldn't lower myself, ol' man,' she said, mimicking his accent.

'You don't have to,' Fitzcuthbert said,

recovering his customary arrogant tone. He was tough, brave; he had medals to prove it. 'I've been told about you. You're Misfit Lil and you're low enough already.'

'Not as low as a sonofabitch who sells his wife's body to repay his debts! For two pins I'd put a bullet in your fat gut.'

Apprehension gripped Fitzcuthbert as she hinted at the extent of what she knew about him. She'd already revealed that afternoon she knew of his association with Cullen Fowler. Then he sneered, clutching again at the remnants of his courage, and added defiantly, 'You wouldn't dare shoot me.'

She said artlessly, 'Why would I need to? There's easier ways to skin an old tomcat.'

'What do you mean?'

'I've got a kinda close friend in that there telegraph office you've been using in town. I could see to it he sent a message to your bosses in London, telling them what you've been up to.

The unwise gambling and suchlike, your lies to the authorities about Indians and an abducted wife. The clerk would be sure to do it for me. He owes me, you might say — prob'ly's hankering for more! Oh yes, mister, I could destroy you less messily than I might with a bullet, though I'm entirely ready to shoot if you oblige me to!'

In the face of her threats, the last shreds of Fitzcuthbert's forced calm were blown away. He was also disconcerted by such overt self-confidence in a woman. In fact, no woman had ever exerted leverage on him like this. In his world, only the Queen of England held the power to command men.

'What is it you want?' he spluttered, swallowing his pride.

So he was giving her the chance to speak, as she'd planned. She told him what she'd tried to tell him when he'd brushed her off at High Meadows.

'I want you should forget about sending a negative report about the High Meadows cattle ranch to its owners across the ocean. I want that you allow Liam and Mary O'Grady the time to make an honest attempt to recoup the ranch's losses. And I insist you release your poor wife Cecilia from any obligation to be a plaything for Cullen Fowler, who in point of fact is the real reason for O'Grady's woes. He trapped him into becoming his tool . . . the exact same way he has you!'

'I don't understand. Cullen Fowler is my friend — '

Lil scoffed. 'Don't make me laugh! Fowler's planted a rough crew at High Meadows. When the time's ripe, the gang'll rustle all that's left that's worth having. You'll have a fine time explaining *that* to your bosses. I'm a hard-riding, gunslinging gal who can stand between you and the stack of trouble you're facing, but only on my terms.'

Fitzcuthbert glared, his harsh breathing audible. 'All right. You have the upper hand. You know where my wife is, don't you? You'll have to return her here straightaway!'

'No. We'll see about that,' Lil said uncompromisingly. 'You don't know the half of this affair, and I don't know yet that I can trust you.'

The Englishman gave her a further, penetrating look. And his anger returned.

'So you're not offering to help me! You're just trying to help yourself. I've heard of women like you, dressing in men's clothes — stealing their wives. You're a tom, tipping the velvet! Well, I'm not playing, bitch, I'm not playing!'

He began to shake as his anger climbed to apoplexy. No doubt he was thinking that Lil was somehow going to keep his wife from him, claiming her affections and cheating him of her fortune.

'I ain't a tom!' Lil said, her own gorge rising. 'You read me wrong, but remember this: you've got yourself in an almighty fix. Do anything to hurt the O'Gradys or Cecilia and you won't get out of it! You've got yourself on a bad spot, Major Stinking Fitzcuthbert!'

'Get out!' Fitzcuthbert repeated.

'I will!' Lil clipped. 'Though it don't mean the matter's finished. Just watch your step!'

She whirled on her heel and stalked out.

But she left bitterly disappointed. She knew she'd been within an ace of securing Fitzcuthbert's cooperation. Then suddenly, unpredictably, the tempers of a moment had whisked agreement away from them and tossed it to the winds.

Now she had no idea what undertakings Fitzcuthbert was prepared to give. Or how he would act.

★　★　★

Cullen Fowler observed Lilian Goodnight's departure from the old Whittaker house. Furrows appeared between the heavy brows over his beady, monkey eyes. He decided to make his own call on ex-Major Albert Fitzcuthbert forthwith.

He wasn't naïve and didn't trust that

his debtor counted him a bosom friend.

Fitzcuthbert had no servants despite occupying one of the grandest houses in Silver Vein. He opened the door to Fowler himself and they went into the front parlour.

A bottle of claret was opened and drinks were poured. The talk was idle chit-chat for some moments, but Fowler knew his host was waiting, apprehensive about what might have brought him here at such a moment, without invitation or apparent cause.

When Fowler thought his victim was adequately discomposed, he bore in.

'Bertie,' he began heavily, 'I'm a man of patience but as you'll 'preciate, there comes a time when it has to run out. We had a certain deal . . .'

Fitzcuthbert flushed. 'I haven't forgotten, Cullen.'

'If I sound harsh it ain't because of too many cigarettes an' too much whiskey. No, sir! It ain't on account of *too much* of anything. A man has other appetites an' they need attending to regular. You un'erstand what I'm saying? What I'm asking is how much longer will you let your wife make me wait for my winnings?'

'Damnit! You know on good authority it's beyond my control. The stupid woman has allowed herself to be carried off who knows where. The army is out looking for her.'

Fowler scowled. 'Don't have nothing on good authority, Bertie. Fact, I suspicion you're holding out on me. You wouldn't like to drive a wanting man plumb loco — make him go off half-cocked, would you?'

'By Jove, no!' Fitzcuthbert said, his eyes large with pleading. 'I know nothing! It's not like that at all!'

'What say I figure it is like that? That these are delaying tactics to accommodate your pretty little woman's high-toned squeamishness?'

Aghast, Fitzcuthbert jumped to his feet, spilling his drink on to his trousers and the carpet yet not seeming to notice.

'I swear that's absurd! I've done

everything I can . . . Curse me if I don't fathom it. Maybe — maybe she's deserted me.'

Fowler nodded his bullet-shaped head. 'I guess that'd be a mite closer to the truth. But you're sweating an' I got a gut feeling it ain't all!' He flexed the heavy-knuckled fingers of his big hands. 'Come across, Bertie, or I'll knock it out of you. You're in cahoots with pesky Lilian Goodnight. I saw her here. She's the go-between for you an' Cecilia. Your milk-sop madam couldn't hide out on her lonesome in this country.'

'No!' Fitzcuthbert squawked, paling. 'It's not like that. I've nothing to do with the wild American girl!'

'Deny it, huh?' Fowler rose, too, and grabbed a bunch of Fitzcuthbert's coat front in his left hand and bunched his right. 'That's a gall!'

'You've got it wrong, old fellah!' Fitzcuthbert bleated.

'Nope! I've gotten it right. I seen it with my own eyes an' I can smell it in your fear.'

With that, Fowler swung his fist into Fitzcuthbert's face, slamming him back against the wall behind.

Fitzcuthbert, though ageing, was no invalid. He had the instincts of a fighting man with military training and a record behind him. He wasn't to be struck with impunity. With a screech of outrage, he rebounded. He was out to avenge himself for the insult and came with fists cocked.

Fowler's cruel eyes narrowed. 'So you want more, huh? Thought your smarmy gent stuff was all show!'

It was no Queensberry rules for Fowler. He came forward to meet the older man, driving his shoulder into him, using his superior bulk, crowding him back again off balance.

But Fitzcuthbert managed to hook his right into Fowler's throat, which checked his rush. As he gagged, Fitzcuthbert pummelled his ribs — one, two; one, two.

It was like punching an iron-hooped barrel.

Fowler straightened and brought up a brutal knee.

Crippling pain sent the breath whistling out of Fitzcuthbert. It could have been only by dint of sheer will-power that he didn't double up and collapse, as Fowler expected, but swung a fist at his face.

The old soldier's latest recovery took Fowler by surprise, and though Fitzcuthbert's knuckles only skidded across his cheek, there was still enough force in the punch to make him reel and trip over the chair on which he'd been sitting, which was still pulled out from the table. He fell on top of it, smashing one of the front legs with his falling weight.

He rolled swiftly, unhurt, and bounced to his feet with the agility of a monkey who'd dropped from a tree. He wasted no breath on the foul cuss-words that sprang to his mind. Face drawn tight by a cold, ruthless anger, he flew at Fitzcuthbert, fists windmilling. He wanted to punish, to maim maybe. It filled his mind to the exclusion of everything else — except, perhaps, having his way with the beautiful Cecilia. How he'd plunder her soft body when this fool of an aged husband coughed up the secret of where he'd hidden her!

Fitzcuthbert was unwise in the savage ways of the West's rough-house fighting, he was old and out of condition, and Fowler was confident he could give him a thorough trouncing.

Enthusiasm for the task gripped him. He battered Fitzcuthbert about the head with hard-knuckled fists. The tough old bastard was still game to dish it out himself though. Fitzcuthbert hit him back once or twice. A hard punch to the mouth split Fowler's inner lip against his teeth and he tasted blood.

Fowler saw red, too, losing the last vestiges of control over his temper.

Incensed, he blocked Fitzcuthbert's next sally with his left forearm, backhanded him across the eyes, exploded a right flush on his jaw. He followed up swiftly, fists hammering, putting his full weight behind his surge.

The time inevitably came when Fitzcuthbert could take no more punishment. His knees buckled; he fought to keep his footing; he shook his head as though to clear it.

Fowler was beside himself with his fury. He didn't let up. He smashed the older man down, bleeding and gasping, one eye closed and visibly swelling.

And when Fitzcuthbert was on the floor — on his side, groaning and shielding his bloodily split and bruised face, all thought of fight abandoned — Fowler used his boots.

He kicked and stomped, forgetful that he needed Fitzcuthbert to talk.

Weary and sore, more angered than sickened by what he'd done, Fowler finally desisted. But it was too late. He realized that punishing Fitzcuthbert to within an inch of life had not been a smart thing to do.

True, he had enough on the old man to make him think twice before lodging a complaint with the useless local peace officer, Sheriff Hamish Howard, but the point was that now he was virtually unconscious, it would possibly be a long while before the man was in a state where he could force him to divulge the whereabouts of his tasty young wife.

It might not be possible at all; once recovered, Fitzcuthbert wouldn't be apt to give him the opportunity to deliver another beating.

With chagrin, Fowler figured he'd overplayed his hand, blown his chance. Yet he was obsessed with the idea of possessing the delicious Cecilia. His blood was on fire for her every time his thoughts dwelled on the time in this house when the loveliness of her had been presented to him, vulnerably, and he'd taken advantage only to have his pleasure broken short . . .

Feeling yet more cheated than before, he went to Fitzcuthbert's kitchen and angrily sloshed water from a pitcher into a basin. He washed away blood and held a wet, cool cloth to his bruises. He straightened his clothing and dabbed at a bloodstain on his cuff.

Engravings of flowers were on the wall, the frames dusty, and a basket of creepers, which hadn't lately been watered, hung from the ceiling. These signs of a woman's touch — and recent neglect — were unwanted reminders of the absent Cecilia.

It seemed he was stymied. But was he?

Fitzcuthbert didn't know he was about to steal a huge and valuable High Meadows herd with the compliance of the O'Gradys, and though Fitzcuthbert maintained he had no arrangement with Misfit Lil, with his own eyes he'd witnessed the girl's visit to his house. Which made Fitzcuthbert's denials hogwash.

By the time Fowler had cleaned himself up and was circumspectly leaving the house, he had a new plan all worked out. His discouragement had gone out with the bloodstained wash water.

It was very obvious really. He still had Fitzcuthbert and Liam O'Grady where he wanted them; where they could do nothing to stop his rustling coup.

Meanwhile, it was also blindingly obvious who could lead him to the hiding place of the object of a lust he would surely consummate. He didn't need Fitzcuthbert, who'd made himself his own worst enemy.

The betrayer of Cecilia would be Misfit Lil!

# 12

## Lone Eagle Mesa

Misfit Lil was riding toward the high pass where the entrance to the Old Horse Thief's Cave was located in the crumbling sandstone cliff face. Providing Cecilia with company and replenishments to her scanty supplies had become a regular chore, eating up all her spare moments at High Meadows.

The sun rode high but she continually felt prickles of cold between her shoulder blades.

Lil had long believed in sixth sense — the eyes she was sure existed in the back of most young women's heads to tell them when they were watched. Real eyes narrowed against the brightness of the blue sky, she looked all around.

She saw nothing except a pair of bald eagles. They climbed high on slow, powerful wing beats, then soared. The eagles' spread wings spanned seven feet and were distinctively marked with a white diagonal line and a spot of white on the underside. Theirs were the only movements Lil could see in any of the surroundings, but her fears were not put to rest. It wasn't eagles' eyes that were on her.

She decided it would be wise to deviate from her route. With skill and luck, she might draw out whoever she was now sure was spying on her from cover.

Circuitously, she descended from the pass. Going through a stretch of timber, she paused to sweep pine needles over her tracks, taking care not to disturb the damp mould beneath and bring it to the surface, which would only create different tell-tale marks.

She trotted Rebel for bleaker parts where the sandstone gave way to grey granite and trees and shrubs were sparser. Still she had the feeling she was being tracked, but she laid a bet with herself that she knew the rock jumble better than her unknown shadower, and won it. Doubling back, she caught sight of a lone rider between the boulders.

It was Red Ballinger!

She thanked the instinct or luck that had prompted her to switch course and lay a false trail. Even so, she was bothered. She'd led Red in the right direction at first. On later consideration, he or someone else might well figure out where she'd deviated and mount a successful search for her original destination. Too, Red was of the outlaw stripe. If he'd been on the dodge sometime, and she reckoned he had, he'd be as familiar with all the tricks for obscuring tracks.

Since she'd made him the laughing-stock of his sidekicks on the first morning at High Meadows, Red had quit the haywire outfit and gone back to Black Dog, rejoining the ranks of the mining camp hangers-on where Cullen Fowler recruited his stooges.

It was Lil's guess that Red was still in

Fowler's employ, trying to find out where Cecilia was holed up. Her heartbeat quickened. Somehow Fowler must have figured Cecilia had help — and that it was hers. Possibly Fitzcuthbert had told him. She began to regret her secretive visit to Silver Vein, but she'd made it with the best intention, to stop the British investors' agent from taking action against Liam O'Grady. Hadn't the duffer understood when she'd told him Fowler was High Meadows's real enemy?

Lil was in a quandary. Sooner or later, Red Ballinger or Fowler would hit on the Old Horse Thief's Cave as a likely place to which she'd been heading.

Cecilia would have to be moved.

Playing for time, Lil led Red on a devious chase. But winding him and his horse would affect herself in the same fashion. It was also plain that in her hurry she couldn't help little things that would give her away to a half-smart tracker: the horsehoe mark in soft dirt here and there, the dislodged stone, the bruised grass stalk, the crushed thistle — none of which she would be able to cover.

She realized she'd have to try something more drastic to shake off Red Ballinger. Something that would delay him. Racking her brains and delving into her detailed memory of the country produced an answer, although a dangerous one.

Lone Eagle Mesa reared high above surrounding features in a wild and isolated stretch of near-wilderness. On the eastern side, white water tumbled through a rugged canyon. The top of the mesa was accessible only to a climber. Maybe she could fool Red into thinking Cecilia was camped up there.

Lil came to the river and sent her surefooted grey cow-pony pounding along its edge and occasionally splashing through the shallows. She crossed the foaming water over a series of large boulders, allowing Rebel to pick his way cautiously on the wet surfaces.

On the far side, shingle and sand formed a narrow margin between the edge of the fast-flowing, greenish river and the base of a high wall of rock. Lil jumped from the saddle and slapped Rebel on the rump to send him toward a clump of yellow aspens where the strip widened out before coming to an abrupt dead-end.

Red Ballinger was not far behind. Daringly, Lil began to climb. The granite rockface reared in solemn majesty hundreds of feet to Lone Eagle's table-top. In most places it was about sheer. Luckily she had no bad head for heights, and hand and footholds were plenty, but she felt like a fly on a wall. Cold sweat dewed her forehead as she went higher.

Once, she looked down at what she'd already scaled, and the river's swirling eddies beneath produced a bout of giddiness. She averted her gaze and clambered up and up.

She was almost to the top when Red's triumphant yell told her he'd come into sight. He thought he had her trapped.

'Hey! Stop, yuh dumb bitch! Yuh can't git away now yuh're afoot, an' I want yuh!'

'I know,' Lil called back jeeringly. 'You tried once before and hurt yourself. Remember?'

She kept climbing rapidly.

★ ★ ★

The punishing, roundabout ride had already taken its toll on Red Ballinger. He savvied Lil Goodnight had caught on she was being followed. She'd been fooling him, teasing him, and the taunt was the last straw. Any moment, Lil would finish her ascent and disappear from his field of vision.

He'd as soon shoot her as let her get away, especially since he figured Cecilia Fitzcuthbert was liable to be up there, on the mesa, and he could complete his mission for Cullen Fowler without needing Misfit Lil any more.

He dismounted, picketed his horse and ran to the rock face, drawing and cocking a long-barrelled pistol. When he thought he'd reached a bench that was close enough, he raised his left forearm level with his eyes, laid the gun barrel across it, took aim, and fired.

★　★　★

A slug ricocheted with an ear-splitting scream off the hard granite several feet from Lil's head.

God, was he trying to kill her?

Lil was a top markswoman and she knew she wasn't within sufficient range of Red for a pistol shot to be reliably effective. She was at least 150 feet distant and he wouldn't find hitting her easy because of his weapon's short sight radius. Moreover, the gun would tend to pull sideways when the trigger was squeezed, even if the barrel was steadied.

But Red might be a better, or luckier, shot than she anticipated. When two more slugs struck the rock face within feet of her, creating terrifying splinter showers of granite, she made a frantic scramble for the top of the mesa.

Breathing hard, peering back over the edge, she saw that Red hadn't given up the pursuit. He'd left the last decent ledge and was climbing up after her.

Red Ballinger was dumber than she'd thought, or so mad at her, he'd gone loco. She didn't aim to exchange gunshots with him. There were easier weapons at hand and he was as vulnerable as she'd been moments before.

It was the work of a moment to shove a huge hunk of rock to the edge of the mesa and over.

It passed close to Red, showering him with the smaller stuff it dislodged. His shrill scream of fury was lost in the solid thump that seemed to go up to the blue sky as the rock crashed on to the river bank and bounced into the rushing water, sending up a great gout into the air.

The echoes rolled like thunder and Red, untouched but enraged, resumed his purposeful climb.

Lil shrugged. Well, she didn't intend to let him get his hateful paws on her again, or put a bullet in her, and he was surely asking for a messy fate.

She sent second and third boulders in the path of the first. And they also caused rumbling rock falls of their own.

Soon, chips of granite were flying every which way and the whole face was hidden by clouds of dust and the great splashes of water flung as much as thirty feet high as the debris plunged into the river.

The ground trembled while the unstoppable rock-slide ran a course. It probably lasted less than two minutes but to Lil it seemed to be for ever. She was white-faced and awestruck at the havoc she'd set in train. Yet her dominating emotion was a strange mingling of anger at the moves being made against her and Cecilia, and elation that she was escaping what

186

surely would have been death or worse at the ruthless hands of Red Ballinger.

When peace returned, she could see no sign of her would-be killer. Red had vanished without trace. Or was that an edge of his broad-brimmed brown hat half-buried by the fallen rocks?

Whatever, no smashed body was sprawled on the rocks or in the rushing river far below. She didn't intend to go looking for one and possibly having to pull it out of the water. At best, she would only be able to cover it with the fallen debris and she didn't much care if wild creatures feasted on his remains.

She was without remorse. Red Ballinger had been a born fool, an ugly, dirty-minded swine who was no loss to the world.

She climbed down from Lone Eagle Mesa. She set the outlaw's horse loose and slapped it on the rump.

'Get outa here! Scat!'

She went to retrieve Rebel. There was no time to waste. Her assistance was needed by the wronged living:

Cecilia Fitzcuthbert. She had to complete the delayed visit with the poor thing, who would surely be worrying about her failure to show.

The only satisfying part of today's exploit was that she'd noted her follower in time. She concluded the need to shift Cecilia to safer, more comfortable lodging was of no greater urgency than before.

# 13

## Dead Man Rides

Just before ten o'clock in the morning, Major Albert Fitzcuthbert put on his top hat and checked his face in the mirror of the mahogany hat-stand in the hallway of the Whittaker mansion. It was pale, haggard and bruised, but the scabs had been cleaned up or hidden with court plaster and his eyes were cold and alert.

He left the house and put his swagger-cane to more practical ends than usual as he limped painfully along Silver Vein's main street to the office of Sheriff Hamish Howard.

His face was taut with apprehension as well as healing wounds. He had no great hope that the sheriff would be of assistance. It was whispered locally that Howard had little interest in righting wrongs or ensuring fair play; that his primary interest lay in exercising the duties of office which facilitated bolstering his own reputation and collecting revenue by way of fees and taxes.

Furthermore, Fitzcuthbert was aware that he couldn't divulge all the background details of the assault he'd suffered at the hands and boots of Cullen Fowler. He'd thought matters through and seen the way the wind was blowing. Fowler had bled him of what money he'd had — which was supplied by his principals to cover the expenses of his High Meadows mission. Unable to collect the unorthodox compensation agreed on in lieu, he was no longer a friend.

He'd also sewn him up damnably.

Fitzcuthbert strained to recall the story told by the queer girl Misfit Lil, which he'd dismissed out of hand. This was that Fowler was preparing to clean out High Meadows in a rustling raid with the enforced co-operation of its manager, Liam O'Grady.

Here was an angle he could ask the sheriff to investigate, keeping dark his own prior transactions with the gambling cattle-buyer.

Howard was in his office with his feet propped on the edge of his boot-scarred desktop and his fat backside firmly planted in a cushioned swivel chair from which he made no attempt to rise.

'Howdy, Mr Fitzcuthbert.'

'Good morning, Sheriff.'

'You cut yourself shavin'?' he asked in a tone of bored indifference.

Fitzcuthbert bared his teeth with horror at the man's lack of respect. His slovenliness grated. If the discipline of the leaders of Her Majesty's loyal forces in India had been allowed to sink to such a low, they would never have overcome the mutinous Nizam Ali Khan.

'Something of that nature, sir, yes.' Then he added heavily, 'But nothing should be permitted to stop a man carrying out his assigned duties with appropriate diligence.'

Howard gave this statement brief contemplation. *Hmm*, he thought, *I ain't stupid, you know — that's a sly dig.* Having expended his energy on this mental feat, what he said was much briefer.

'Oh?'

'I came to make a statement, Sheriff.'

The feet stayed on the desk; the backside on the chair. 'In regards to what?'

'I understand the High Meadows cattle are to be stolen — rustled, as you might say — with the connivance of the range-boss, Liam O'Grady. I'm told the thieves will run off a big herd as soon as conditions are propitious.'

'I see . . . ' Howard said, though he didn't and it sounded like Fitzcuthbert might be working around to asking him to take some action, do some work, which went against his grain. 'Where did yuh hear this?'

'I was informed by a Miss Lilian Goodnight.'

Howard's relief was visible. He sank

lower in his chair.

'I might a' knowed! Oh, we know all 'bout *her* in these parts. She's a reg'lar teller of windies an' a born trouble-maker. Pay no nevermind to *her*, the li'l slut!'

'Does that mean you aren't going to do anything?'

'Cuss me if I know what I can do, mister. You want I should guard the HM cows personal on account o' what Misfit Lil says? Not on your life! I ain't wastin' no time like that, none what-ever!'

'So what must I do?'

'Yuh can do what yuh wants,' Howard said dismissively. 'I bet a stack o' greenbacks it's moonshine.'

'Very well, sir. Perhaps I shall have to take my report elsewhere.'

'Sure. Yuh do that — yuh take it anyplace yuh like. So long, an' good luck.'

Fitzcuthbert left muttering. This was a fine note. The sheriff was an utter fool!

Though he felt deucedly rotten, he had to do something to try to retrieve his crumbling situation; to salvage what he could. Where to next?

* * *

As it was approaching full moon, Misfit Lil adopted a new strategy, visiting Cecilia at the Old Horse Thief's Cave after it had risen. On a clear night, in the strong but eerie light, she hid Rebel in buckbrush and hunkered with the Englishwoman beside the cave entrance. The feel of the rock was hard and cold against their backs despite the thickness of clothing and the blankets Lil had brought out on a previous visit.

'This place is scary, clammy, shivery. I don't like it,' Cecilia complained. 'Perhaps I should go back to my husband, beg his forgiveness for runn — '

They were close together and Lil gripped her arm, almost hissing.

'Listen, Cecilia. Listen! You can't go back. In my book, a woman has the right to choose who she lies with. Fitzcuthbert is a skunk who'd take even that away from you, let alone the inheritance set to become his property on account of your being his wife. He's rotten. You have to leave him for good. Go some place else.'

Cecilia wailed in distress. 'Where, Lil?'

'I don't know yet, but I'll come up with something.' She pulled out a half-empty bottle of Very Old Scotch Whisky. 'Want a swig?'

Cecilia's shoulders shuddered delicately. 'No, thank you.'

Lil unstoppered the bottle, put it to her lips and gulped.

'I'll have to ask my friend, Jackson Farraday,' she went on a mite ambiguously. 'He's a very educated man as well as a frontiersman ... speaks seven languages and heaps of Indian lingoes ... knows most everything. He'll help you break free and start afresh, I swear.'

Cecilia bit her lip and shook her head violently.

'That only sounds fine in theory! And Indian culture has no lessons for a white woman. Their women are depraved and promiscuous. I've read what our clerics and professors say. Before the white man came they had orgiastic fertility rites and danced, naked and singing, around erotic emblems.'

Lil snorted her derision. 'The old friars got it wrong: what they witnessed was true divinity not depravity. But the damnfool sky pilots bulled ahead and preached their European ways, the morality of male-dominated marriage and female sexual shame!'

'Oh, I mustn't argue with you, dear Lil,' Cecilia sighed. 'You're my only friend. It's just that I don't think you know what's to be done.'

But Lil was stubborn. 'Hell, Jackson's brain will be teeming with possibilities, I bet. I didn't say you had to turn Indian! Ain't it common knowledge many young Eastern women, ostracized by their families and communities, travel west and start their lives over again? They change their names, fabricate new backgrounds.'

'Major Fitzcuthbert says the single women who come West unaccompanied become prostitutes. That all women are whores by nature anyw — '

Lil suddenly stiffened and put a hand to Cecilia's lips.

'*Shh*! What was that?' she whispered.

'I heard nothing,' Cecilia whispered back, trembling.

But a faint rumbling of fast-approaching hoofs grew louder.

'Into the cave! Hide yourself!' Lil said urgently. It was too late for them to flee. She took Cecilia's pretty face between her hands as a mother might a child's and pressed a quick kiss on her lips. 'Be brave!' she said, and pushed her into the darkness.

The beat of confidently ridden broncs grew louder, then four horsemen swept into view — at first a line of shadows, near-black silhouettes against the starlit night sky.

As they rode up, the puzzle of who they were was quickly settled.

'What do you know?' Lil muttered. 'These gents are Cullen Fowler and a bunch of his rogue helpers. Damned if I know how they found us, but we got bad trouble!'

'Hey, you! Lil Goodnight, you bitch!' one of the arrivals yelled. 'Give up! Hoist your hands an' come outa there!'

More disconcerting to Lil than the actual orders was the identity of their caller. It was Red Ballinger!

'But you're supposed to be dead, you bastard!' she said.

Cullen Fowler laughed at her. 'The supposing's wrong, gal! You may've thought what you did at Lone Eagle Mesa was smart, but Red fell in the river an' was carried downstream, alive! Shoulda checked, huh?'

'How did you find me? What do you want?'

Lil was reckoning the odds, playing for time. She could work out for herself the answers to her questions.

'I can guess what Red wants,' Fowler said. 'I'm gonna claim my owings — Cecilia Fitzcuthbert first, then all the stock that's left on High Meadows. Your hideout weren't so difficult to locate. Red knew where you started on giving him the run-around. It ain't so far from Silver Vein an' we just had to go through the likely spots — *Hey, what are you doing?*'

Lil made a sudden dive and simultaneously what she figured had to be the fastest draw of her life. Or her last. As she hit the ground, she cocked the Colt. It was no time for fancy marksmanship. Rolling — without aiming — she fired the gun on an extended arm in the general direction of Fowler's body mass.

Though startling, and unexpected in its daring, the move was only partly successful. Fowler pulled his horse back and aside. The bullet that should have buried itself in the broad target of his fleshy thigh, hit the animal in the neck. It dropped from under him, but he managed to jerk his feet free from the stirrups as it sank and threw himself behind it.

'Kill her! Shoot, you fools!' he bellowed.

But his henchmen were stunned by the speed of Lil's reckless actions and deafened by the piteous squealing of the stricken, dying horse.

And Lil wasn't finished. In short order, Red Ballinger lost the use of his drawn gun. His horse was rearing on its hind legs in alarm and Lil was able to disarm him with a second shot, which broke his wrist. He swore luridly.

The man to the right of Fowler, rightly judging that shooting from the back of a spooked horse was going to be impractical, swung from leather, but Lil ran at him, bringing him down as he hit the ground, then booting his gun out of his hand and away into the darkness.

Fowler rose from behind the protection of his dead horse and shot. In his agitation, he shot too quickly and the slug, instead of hitting Lil, ploughed into the dismounted and unarmed man's chest, tearing a fatal hole through him.

'Shit!' Fowler said. He wasn't sorrowful; he was exasperated.

The fourth man, hardcase though he looked, was more cautious and didn't have the stomach for what was disintegrating into a bloody hash of a job. He jammed spurs into his horse's sides and lit out.

Red Ballinger had also now dismounted and found his fallen gun. He advanced on Lil, gripping it in his good hand.

'We don't need the others,' Fowler gritted. 'She's your meat, Red!' Exultation came into his voice. 'I'm going to fetch out the other sweet thing!'

'You can't put me down left-handed!' Lil told Red warningly.

'You jest see if I can't!' Red howled.

'Huh! You've tried to kill me afore . . . try to make that gun smoke and your brave words'll be your last!'

Lil's wiry body moved with all the flowing, quiet grace of a big cat. She tensed in a crouch, alert and ready to fire the moment Red made his play.

Red Ballinger's eyes were bloodshoot and murderous, but he was rattled, too. He'd heard about this slut's prowess with a gun. What was it they called her hereabouts? The Princess of Pistoleers . . .

He hesitated a moment, then with a foolish grunt that telegraphed his moment of decision, he lifted his six-shooter, hurling himself to one side.

Two shots smashed echoingly, shattering again the calm of the moonlit night. One whipped past Lil, wild and wide. Red was hit and he staggered, but kept coming with a dimwitted doggedness.

Lil fired again, the roar of her gun surging out to be flung back by the sandstone sides of the upland pass. And Red was still on his feet, though Lil was sure she hadn't missed.

She knew she had four empty shells in her Colt. She had one shot left. Swaying, Red lifted his left, gun-filled hand, hardly aware of what he was doing.

Nostrils quivering, her grey gaze cold as ice, Lil shot him in the head. The heavy .45 slug split his bushy red eyebrows and he toppled full-length at her feet, his face in the dust, his ruined head splashing blood on her boots.

Meanwhile, Fowler, assuming Lil was guaranteed to meet her comeuppance, had rushed into the cave. He came out as the echoes of the gunfight faded and the powder-smoke drifted like white fog on the night air. With him, he dragged Cecilia, white-faced and whimpering.

Fowler had expected to see Misfit Lil dead. It dawned on him that instead it was his small gang which had been wiped out. He was shocked. But with his prize in hand, he was also undismayed. He promptly pulled Cecilia close to him and drew a knife. It glinted as he laid it across her neck.

'You gun-crazy, blood-crazy tyke! Well, you ain't stopping me . . . make one false step an' I'll slit your friend's goddamn lilywhite throat!'

# 14

## Beauty and The Beast

Cecilia made no effort to oppose Fowler as he boosted her on to the horse of the man he'd shot. His threats had effectively cowered her into meek submission.

'Just what gives you any right to carry Mrs Fitzcuthbert away, Fowler?' Lil demanded.

'Permission was granted me by her lawful husband. She ain't got no right to be here — nor you to be bringing her chow an' stuff.'

'Where are you taking her?'

Fowler sneered victoriously. 'That ain't for you to know, sticky beak. To a place where no nevermind is paid to a woman's screams!'

Lil could do nothing. Her gun was empty and to attempt to reload it, confirming her helplessness to stop him, would be stark staring, fatally mad.

'What are you going to do to her?'

Fowler's leer widened. 'You do ask dumb questions, missy! I'll take what's owing me — an' your pretty friend'll l'arn to like it, have no fear 'bout that.'

In Lil's eyes, the 'it' was rape; no justification of an entitled husband's say-so would serve to make it anything different.

'She won't like it! She never could!'

'Once she falls to me, she'll fall! There's no bounds to a female once she's gotten the taste. Ask any whore . . . it's the way of it!'

He was taunting her, rubbing salt into the wound with his cynicism, but Lil was incapable of restraining her anger.

'You know that you lie!' she burst out. 'You lie, lie, lie!'

Tears came to her eyes. She was devastated by the horror of Cecilia's seizure. It was wicked that such degenerate crimes could be perpetrated, even in the world's most lawless places. Fowler was sub-human, an animal, a beast; Cecilia was delicate, a fragile, fairy beauty. What Fowler had in mind for her would desecrate and destroy the Cecilia Lil had quickly grown to love despite their huge differences.

Transfixed, she was obliged to watch as he swiftly slashed Red Ballinger's loose horse with trailing rein ends. 'Git!' he barked. With an affronted whinny, the bronc galloped away.

He mounted up behind the stiff and frightened Cecilia, whose only sound was the chattering of her teeth.

'An' I know where your cayuse is, kid,' Fowler told Lil. 'Picketed in that clump of cedars. It won't be there any more'n the instant it takes to stampede it likewise. So don't reckon you can follow me!'

He kicked his mount with his heels, took a tighter, crueller hold on Cecilia, and off he went.

The clatter of hoofs and some weak

cries of alarm from Cecilia, who was unused to being on horseback, receded and an electric silence returned to the environs of the Old Horse Thief's Cave.

Lil had few qualms about Rebel. She'd known her grey cow-pony from a foal and he was trained well. A few whistles would bring him back from wherever he was forced to flee, which wouldn't be far.

But when she thought about her chances of saving Cecilia, she felt sick. By the time she was ready to go after Fowler, he'd have a huge lead. Her tracking skills were second to none — bar Jackson Farraday's — but only daybreak would create sufficient light to bring them to bear rapidly.

She went over to Fowler's dead horse, but found it carried no saddle-bags which might contain clues to where he was currently hanging out and might be returning to subject his victim to his vileness.

She was picking her way through the jumbled boulders towards the twisted

cedars, when the significance of something she'd subconsciously spotted
registered. In a few quick strides, she
was back beside the fallen horse.

It was just as she'd thought. Visible
on the offside stirrup iron were traces of
paint . . . pink, or was it scarlet? The
moonlight was deceptive, but Lil was
sure she'd seen such distinctive paint
before, and recently. The iron had scraped
against something freshly painted.

Where? And would the answer tell
her in what direction she had to ride
— pronto — to rescue Cecilia from her
barbaric fate?

Lil set her brain to thinking, hard.

★　★　★

Major Albert Fitzcuthbert took his
woes to Fort Dennis in a bid to salvage
what he could of the precarious
circumstances in which he had landed
himself. Though it was far from India,
scene of the highlights of his past
military career, something about the

fort was familiar to him, comforting. Possibly it was the austerity of military outposts common the world over.

The fluttering colours, the clean, open expanse of the parade ground, so different from the wind-blown litter and clutter in Silver Vein, were features that lifted his sagging spirits.

A sentry who met him at the massive wooden gates escorted him past a mix of log blockhouses — housing the men's barracks, the stables, a black-smith's shop and the mess shack — and on to the administration block, which, like the officers' quarters, the infirmary, a commissary and the guardhouse, was a solid stone structure.

He was ushered into the presence of Lieutenant Michael Covington, the very young man with whom he felt he'd struck up an instant rapport on the occasion of the Indian attack on the stagecoach.

He put down his swagger-cane ceremoniously on the young lieuten-ant's desk, set himself in the offered seat and told as much of his story as he dared. He finished his report with as much dramatic flourish as he was able.

'So you see, I suspect that — er — certain forces, shall we say, are about to rob the people I represent, who have unsuspectingly invested their money, their life savings perhaps, in the great American cattle industry. The military must intervene.'

But Covington's sympathy was not forthcoming.

'A fine notion, Major. Please tell, what is the result you want us to achieve?'

'Why, sir, to apprehend the villains!'

'It all sounds very vague, Major, and the suggested remedy is high-handed, quite outside the jurisdiction of the United States Army. I was most sorry previously, when we had your report of how your wife had been kidnapped, possibly by native hostiles. We searched high and low for her. At great length and expense, I might add. Nothing was revealed that bore out your claims, and sadly, there was no trace of your good lady. This latest calamity afflicting you sounds no less mysterious and fantastical. I suggest you return to Sheriff Hamish Howard, who is the civilian law, and present him with more complete details.'

'But the man is a nincompoop!'

Covington said, 'All the more reason for us not to make the same of hard-working troopers.'

'Now look here!' Fitzcuthbert spluttered, as soon as he'd digested the oblique comment. 'I think that's going too far. Can I talk to that scout fellah of yours — Jackson somebody?'

Covington said he meant Jackson Farraday and arranged it.

The scout, who was not enlisted in the military though he worked for them, listened with deeper interest. He frowned frequently and probed disturbingly for the sources of his knowledge of a planned rustling raid.

Fitzcuthbert thought he hedged — lied, rather — cleverly.

'Oh, I hear there's a gang gathering in a place called Black Dog. There's a crooked cattle-buyer called Fowler. It's voiced about in the Silver Vein saloons.'

Jackson Farraday nodded sagely. 'So are many things. I'll see what I can do. I'll speak with the commanding officer here, Colonel Brook Lexborough, but I hold out no hopes. Remember, the company here has only recently explored the notion that Mrs Fitzcuthbert was snatched by reservation jumpers. That was always imaginative to my mind. These fresh accusations could prove equally groundless and time-wasting.'

'Thank you for your candour, Mr Farraday,' Fitzcuthbert said stiffly.

With no promise of instant help from the cavalry, he left the fort in a mood of frantic despondency. His money and Cecilia were gone. He stood to lose everything: reputation, his commission from the cattle syndicate in London, his livelihood and possibly the fortune that was to come through his wife.

All he could do was take direct,

physical action for which he knew deep down he was no longer really fit.

Cullen Fowler's lair was at Black Dog. He must obtain a horse and ride at speed to the mining camp and find and destroy the blasted man. Only thus might he foil the impending rustling raid single-handed and restore himself in his principals' eyes.

It was a tall order, but one failing an old British Army soldier didn't have was cowardice . . .

\* \* \*

It was once written of a Wild West town that 'it had reared its flimsy buildings in the face of God and rioted day and night with no thought of reckoning; mad, insane with hellishness unlimited'.

Much the same could be said of the burgeoning mining community of Black Dog. It was a hell-hole that desperadoes of all stripes used as a happy hunting-ground. They came there to prey on the honest suckers and greenhorns drawn by the promise of mineral wealth.

But Misfit Lil came this time to look for scarlet paint.

For she'd remembered where she'd last seen the stuff. It was when she'd ridden into Black Dog to help Liam O'Grady rescue his Mary from the hands of the unknown whoremonger who owned the Great Western Hotel. The garish stuff had been crudely and hurriedly splashed on the new building's unseasoned white pine exterior, including the lumber of the rails and posts.

The night was in its dying hours but an oil lantern burned over a door back of the hotel; other light showed at several upstairs windows and it was clear pleasure, or business, of a sort was still being transacted.

Lil gave the door a loud and authoritative hammering.

A woman's voice called wheezily, 'Who's that?'

Lil said nothing. She hammered some more.

She recognized the voice as Aggie Ryan's. The woman managed the hotel, but she wasn't the mysterious proprietor who'd financed it. Lil was beginning to suspect this was no less than Cullen Fowler himself.

He was an excellent candidate. A whorehouse was exactly the sort of nefarious venture into which he would sink his ill-gotten money in expectation of making more.

Shuffling footsteps and grumbling and coughing within preceded the drawing of a bolt and the turning of a key in a sturdy lock.

The door opened to reveal Aggie Ryan, wearing an old and shapeless flannel dressing-gown over clothes that weren't conventional night attire.

Aggie was a blonde of what might be termed a certain age — the only certain part being that it was no longer young. She had pear-shaped breasts pushed up high with the help of whalebone and her unnatural gold hair was put up in a pile on the back of her head.

'What the hell's wrong, a-hammerin' on my door this time o' night? You want a woman or a drink, feller, you're way too — '

She broke off as she realized that despite the fringed buckskin coat and pants, the caller was a woman.

'Here! I swear you're the trouble-maker that come stirrin' the ruckus over Mary O'Grady. What do you want?'

'I'm coming in to see Cullen Fowler!' Lil replied sharply. 'I know he's here!'

'Oh, he is, is he?' Aggie wheezed, not thinking or bothering to deny the charge. 'Maybe he's in bed and asleep. Won't the mornin' do?'

'No! If he is in bed, he ain't sharing it with bedbugs. Morning will be too late.'

Aggie bristled. 'I don't like your tone, missy. We don't need your kind here. I'm shuttin' up.'

Lil swiftly planted her foot in front of the closing door and leaned against it. She also pulled a gun.

'Hey, missy, you can't do that,' Aggie

216

protested. 'Mr Fowler will be plumb mad at me if'n I let you in!'

'Won't be any madder than I'll be if you keep me out!'

Pallor flecked Aggie's cheeks as she lost the battle to close the door.

'You'll get us both horse-whipped!' she complained, but then she steadied somewhat, watching with clear and calculating eyes.

'I can't stop you. You're so brave. Forcin' your way in with a gun on a defenceless woman . . . '

Lil caught on too late. The sudden change in the woman's demeanour had to have a reason.

She whipped round and saw the face of the man who'd come up behind her without warning as a blur. She had time only to register it was Major Fitzcuthbert. Then with a whistle and a mighty crack like the sound of splitting wood, his swinging cane cut her cruelly across the face.

Her head seemed to explode with pain. She could see nothing except an unbroken curtain of red.

'Get out of my way, the pair of you!' Fitzcuthbert roared, flourishing his hefty rod. 'Or I'll thrash you to shreds!'

Blinded, staggering, Lil lost hold of her gun and her footing and sprawled downwards, gasping for breath. Although she was very dizzy, she realized the madman who'd attacked her was ready to strike again, careless of where and on whom his vicious weapon fell.

Could she dare regain her feet and stand up to him and the torture of another blow?

# 15

## Hellfire at Black Dog

Misfit Lil rolled over twice, to get away from the door and further attack. Stones dug into her back and she scraped her arm, but she wasn't aware of the pain. Her worst and most frightening injury was that the swipe of the cane across her face had left her with impaired vision.

She heard scuffling and a small cry of despair from Aggie Ryan.

It was several moments before Lil could get her breath and rise from behind the trash barrel where she was huddled. Even then, her face was still stinging and her eyes watering. She was convinced a blazing red weal must be striped across the side of her head, the bridge of her nose and her eyelids, where the cane had struck. The slash could have permanently blinded her but luckily hadn't. She held her face to her sleeve, letting it mop up the tears.

Finally, blearily, she stood up and took in the situation.

Aggie Ryan was in an undignified and indignant heap in her doorway.

'He pushed me over, the son of a bitch!'

'Where's he gone?' Lil demanded.

With the defences breached, the brothel madam forgot or put aside her previous objections to Lil's entry.

'Upstairs, front — to Cullen Fowler's private rooms.'

Lil swore and retrieved her gun. 'Ain't nothing for it but to go after him!'

'How come it's any concern o' yours, gal?' Aggie said. 'The Englishman said the woman Fowler's pokin' is his. Let the fools scrap over their hussy like a dog over a bone! It ain't our fight now. None of it.'

Lil's heart sank and her fears deepened. So she had found Cecilia

Fitzcuthbert. She took stairs two at a time.

'I wouldn't go up thar if I was you!' Aggie rasped after her. 'A gal's a fool to mess with rabid critters . . . '

But Lil had come too far to turn back. She knew now what Fowler had meant when he'd said he was taking his hostage to a place where her screams wouldn't be out of place and would be ignored. She had the whole boiling figured out, and she had a mission. To rescue Cecilia . . .

Lil reached the upper landing. Voices came from a room with a partly open door. They were raised in argument.

★   ★   ★

Fitzcuthbert said, 'I'm finished with you, Cullen Fowler, you swine!'

'That's rich, Major . . . Our bargain was plain an' we're not square till I've collected the debts!'

'I see you're working on that,' Fitzcuthbert said acidly.

'Wasn't that the deal . . . or wasn't it?'

'Robbing High Meadows blind and ruining me wasn't!'

'Your money ran dry an' the cattle was the real stakes anyhow. Howsoever, I don't say your woman ain't 'preciated. She's a mighty fancy lady. Mebbe I'll warm her up yet to the notion you Englishmen call a St George. Real looker with no clothes, ain't she? A man could grow fond of her . . . '

'She's my wife, damnit!'

Fowler tutted. 'Well, now, if that ain't what beats all! Don't seem right to me why a young woman like your'n would settle for an ol'-timer. She oughta known you was long drained dry by the succulent houris of the Far East. I heared tell them women shave their mounds an' take a clean sweep underneath. Is that right, Major?'

'My wife is betraying me!' Fitzcuthbert roared, forgetful of his own initiation of the process and Cecilia's horrified opposition. 'I ought to kill you both!'

Cecilia whimpered, 'I resisted his

liberties, Husband! On my honour, I swooned away. I'd never accept the horrid beast!'

'Honour!' Fowler scorned her. 'Honour! Why, you ain't no innocent virgin; you're a married woman an' a nat'ral-born wanton. Forget the fit of fine-lady screams! Tell your idiot major the truth — how your quivering body was answering every shove soon enough — how it was needful from abstinence an' couldn't stop from running the course till ev'ry breath came in a mighty gasp!'

Fitzcuthbert shrilled, 'You bastard, Fowler!' Then, to Cecilia: 'So much, dear Wife, for your silly desertion!'

Cecilia dropped her face but contested his scorn with a jerky cry. 'Any woman who'd had to live with you and knew what you tried to make of me would understand!'

From a neighbouring room a man bellowed, 'Shuddup, will yuh?' and a woman asked sleepily, querulously, 'What is it, Jake?'

★  ★  ★

Through the half-open door, Lil glimpsed a dresser on which sat a lighted lamp. Beside it was Fitzcuthbert's nasty swagger-cane.

It was an occasion for Lil to show her remarkably cool and brave nature. The discarded cane and the unpleasant, stalemated conversation suggested to her, ominously, that Fitzcuthbert must have an alternative, more deadly weapon in his hand: probably a firearm.

Summoning the rare courage that set her aside from others, she rushed in on a confrontation which was much as she'd surmised.

The room was an extravagant, sumptuously furnished affair in comparison with those Lil had entered when she'd come here with Liam O'Grady. It appeared to be a parlour-cum-bedroom. There were rich red drapes, three cushioned upright chairs, a wardrobe, a small writing-desk, the oak dresser and a large double-bed.

Cecilia was on the high bed, trying to cover herself with a crumpled white sheet. Items of her clothing were scattered on an expensive Axminster carpet.

Cullen Fowler was beside one of the chairs, which was on its side and looked as though it might have been knocked over as he jumped off the bed. He wore only his longjohns and these were not buttoned. Lil hadn't seen a man with body hair more profuse. To Cecilia, familiar with none but her husband, having him on top of her, inside her, would have seemed like forced mating with a wild animal.

Albert Fitzcuthbert, with his back to the door, menaced Fowler with a stubby revolver. Lil had seen only one of its like before. It had been called a Webley by its owner, a cowpoke who was the black sheep of a noble British family and who received remittances from home. The gun was a recent, 1870s invention — a top-break, six-shot, double-action revolver with a four-inch barrel. The shape of the barrel and frame, with lock lever on the left of the frame and V-shaped lock spring at the right, was very distinctive.

'I've told the law and the military about your rustling plans, Fowler,' Fitzcuthbert was saying. 'Your cheating days are numbered.'

'Hold your hosses, Major!' Fowler said, smiling a crooked smile. 'The law is Sheriff Howard an' he listens to my say-so, 'cause I pay him taxes, see? An' mebbeso it ain't fitting for the army to interfere.'

When Lil surged in — audaciously, unexpectedly, pushing the door back to crash against the wall — Fitzcuthbert instinctively made a half-turn toward her.

The distraction was all the chance Fowler needed — a lucky break that wouldn't be repeated. As the pointing Webley veered, he dived toward the desk, tore open the drawer and dragged out a revolver of his own, a longer-barrelled Colt. His broad, ugly face was twisted into a grin of pure hate.

The turning point of the game had arrived. The men's guns blazed and crashed in the same instant.

Fowler was on the move and his shot missed Fitzcuthbert. It lodged in the wall, making a small cloud and a trickle of plaster.

Fitzcuthbert was bemused as his thought processes tried to catch up with the rapidity of the action. But Fowler kept right on moving, diving across the big bed. He disappeared behind it and Cecilia rolled or was pulled on top of him.

Had Fitzcuthbert winged or killed Fowler? Lil couldn't tell. As was common in any shooting affray, the measure of confusion and deceptive impressions was large.

Outside the room, more angry shouts were raised, then doors started to open, to be followed by the crash of feet on the stairs — running feet — as the mainly male guests and their female company decamped. It wasn't healthy to stay in such establishments when lead started to fly.

No one attempted to enter Fowler's room. Lil noted fleetingly that a succession of scared, white faces passed the open door with scarcely a pause.

Fitzcuthbert shouted exultantly and furiously at the man who'd ruined him and taken captive his heiress wife.

'You yellow-bellied cur, Fowler; thought you could outsmart me, eh? Well, I can shoot, too, and your rustling coups and gambling tricks are over!'

But Lil knew there was no knowing that they were — yet. Hidden behind the big bed, was Cullen Fowler hunkered down and still scheming?

He could be waiting for the moment when his adversary would drop his defences and be lured towards him, setting himself up to be shot down at point-blank range.

The same thought evidently struck Fitzcuthbert. To her horror, he emptied his gun rapidly and indiscriminately in the direction of the bed, then he broke open the two-piece frame.

The forward end hinged down. The ejector was actuated automatically, simultaneously removing all six cases from the cylinder. Fitzcuthbert groped in his pocket for more cartridges.

'No!' Lil cried. 'Your wife's behind there with Fowler. They'll *both* be killed. Give me the gun!'

Fitzcuthbert swung to face her. He was high-coloured with rage. Or madness.

'I'll give you what's in it!'

'But I'll shoot faster and straighter!' Lil said, knowing the claim might be irrelevant besides rash. In such a confined space, an exchange of gunfire was liable to end in tragedy for all parties.

'Any time you're ready, bitch!'

What happened next was completely unexpected by either of them.

Before Fitzcuthbert or Lil could fire, Cecilia rose from behind the bed. She was naked, but more startlingly she clutched a big gun in both her small hands and she squeezed the trigger.

At close range she couldn't miss, though the gun bucked and its recoil, which she hadn't known to anticipate, threw her back in a heap into the hiding from where she'd emerged.

Fitzcuthbert was back-shot and the slug passed through him and emerged from his belly in an explosion of blood and bits of gut and fabric. He screamed once, shrilly as a horse. The Webley dropped from his grasp with a thud and he stumbled toward Lil, ashen-faced, clutching himself as though trying to hold in his contents. Spurting blood and other stuff forced itself out horrifically between his fingers.

Lil saw the beads of sweat on his upper lip and his forehead. His temples were drenched with it. In this state, without top-hat and swagger-cane, he looked pitiful. As Lil backed from him, his knees gave way slowly until they collapsed quite suddenly and let him down on his face.

Dead.

Lil went around him, barely suppressing a shudder though she wasn't a squeamish person and had seen a peck of ugly demises in her time, which in the scale of lifetimes was still short.

Cecilia was crouched beside the corpse of Cullen Fowler, who had indeed been hit by Fitzcuthbert's first shot. She'd stumbled backwards over him when she'd fired the gun, which proved to be Fowler's Colt. She was sobbing wretchedly.

'You killed Fitzcuthbert, Cecilia,' Lil said. 'Shot your husband in the back. Why did you do that?'

'He was going to kill *you!*' she moaned. 'I don't care. I hated him! I love you!'

Misfit Lil said nothing, but figured swiftly. This was a hell of a note. Two dead men in a hotel room to be explained away, and a woman she considered innocent professing to love her. Should a case be made out from the evidence, and weighed up before a frontier jury, the outcome was unlikely to be justice, albeit she'd once seen the concept represented as a blindfolded lady.

She decided the probing questions which were going to be asked — the possible conclusions and charges following from an examination of the scene — wouldn't serve Cecilia's best interests. She'd been sorely wronged enough.

'We must get out fast and burn this foul place and all its contents down,' she declared abruptly. 'Put on your clothes, Cecilia! Time's a-wasting . . . '

She took the oil lamp from the dresser, blew it out, and in the gloom began sloshing its contents over the bed and the two men's bodies.

'This is madness, Lil,' Cecilia said as she dressed compliantly. 'Other people will get hurt.'

'No, they won't. The place is good as empty. First sign of trouble, the whores and their customers took off like scalded cats!'

Lil didn't know this for a fact, but

she knew it would sound reassuring to her companion.

In the event, the fire went badly wrong — or, as Lil later decided, incredibly right. It took hold quickly and jumped from the euphemistically named Grand Western Hotel to the neighbouring ramshackle frame buildings and shacks.

More buildings began to burn, then still others in rapid succession.

Lil and Cecilia fled down the main street, outrunning the leaping yellow glow that was lighting up the place like day. The close-packed stores and houses were quickly being absorbed into a single, continuous, nightmarish inferno. All around, the panicking people of the hastily built and unlovely mining camp ran with them in states of half-dress and shouting confusion.

Some called out for separated companions or loved ones like lost souls.

'Catherine!'

'Sid! Where are you?'

The uproar ceased only at daybreak.

At this juncture, bugle blasts were heard on the smoky air and the cavalry dashed belatedly on to the scene.

* * *

Jackson Farraday was with Lieutenant Michael Covington when the troop arrived in the smouldering, charred remains of the settlement.

'A very Black Dog, Mr Covington.'

The scout had managed to talk Fort Dennis into following up the wild reports made by Major Albert Fitzcuthbert.

Covington scowled. 'I don't think we'll find any rustling gang here.'

'But look!' Jackson cried, pointing. 'Isn't that Miss Goodnight and the missing Mrs Fitzcuthbert?'

They rode across the ruins to the young women.

Misfit Lil told them she didn't know the present whereabouts of Major Fitzcuthbert or about his accusations against Cullen Fowler.

'Think I saw 'em at the hotel where the fire started. Maybe they had an argument, shot each other . . . ' She shrugged. 'Who will ever know?'

Covington was suspicious. 'Hmm! You usually you have a smart answer for everything.'

'Sure.' She produced a bottle of whiskey she'd grabbed from behind the bar as she'd left the fired hotel. 'A drink. Come on, have a drop of whiskey on me!'

'Lil!' Jackson chided. 'You ought to know better.'

Lil sighed, lifted the bottle and studied its amber contents. 'But they do call it the panacea for all ills and sorrows. Also good for loosening up the stuffing in a shirt.'

Covington swallowed the teasing and snapped, 'You're prevaricating! What about this fire? Do you know how it happened?'

'Can't say as I do, Mike. Damnedest thing I ever saw! This place needed cleaning up real bad. And now it has been, right and proper. Nothing purifies like fire.'

'It isn't like you to know nothing, Miss Goodnight,' Covington said.

'Ain't it now? Well, you'll just have to believe it.'

Later, Lil told Jackson that Fitzcuthbert's death left Cecilia free to live a life of her own and enjoy an inheritance. Also satisfactorily, Liam O'Grady's potential accusers were dead and he had a fresh chance to straighten out the affairs of High Meadows.

'Fowler and Fitzcuthbert went up in the flames and Hell will be even hotter for 'em!'

Jackson frowned. 'I think you do know more.'

Lil went silent.

'Haven't lost your tongue, have you?'

'No,' Lil said. 'Just guarding it.'

We do hope that you have enjoyed reading this large print book.

Did you know that all of our titles are available for purchase?

We publish a wide range of high quality large print books including:
**Romances, Mysteries, Classics**
**General Fiction**
**Non Fiction and Westerns**

Special interest titles available in large print are:
**The Little Oxford Dictionary**
**Music Book, Song Book**
**Hymn Book, Service Book**

Also available from us courtesy of Oxford University Press:
**Young Readers' Dictionary**
**(large print edition)**
**Young Readers' Thesaurus**
**(large print edition)**

For further information or a free brochure, please contact us at:
**Ulverscroft Large Print Books Ltd.,**
**The Green, Bradgate Road, Anstey,**
**Leicester, LE7 7FU, England.**
**Tel:** (00 44) **0116 236 4325**
**Fax:** (00 44) **0116 234 0205**

*Other titles in the*
*Linford Western Library:*

## LAWMEN

### Jack Giles

Tom Ford, the sheriff of Stanton, was gunned down while trying to keep the peace between the hands of rival ranches. News of Tom Ford's death reaches his son, Chris, and Marshal Sam Ward while they are hunting down a killer. Chris returns home to face his past and to find his father's killer and for this he must take up his father's badge — only to discover that not everything is as it seems . . .

# BLOOD CREEK

## Lance Howard

Fifteen years earlier five unruly sons had committed a heinous crime against a young Ute woman, and walked away unpunished. But now a ruthless killer is stalking those boys. Bent on revenge he's murdering their wives and, piece by piece, destroying their lives. After manhunter Calin Travers is attacked, then lured to Sundown, Colorado, he discovers himself face to face with guilt from the past and a vengeful killer who has marked him for death.

# KID DYNAMITE

## Michael D. George

Government agent Scott Taylor arrives in Adobe Wells to tackle the corruption which is rife. But Cody Carter has other plans. He's ruled Franklin County for years with an army of outlaws and Cheyenne warriors to do his killing for him. Forewarned of Taylor's mission, Carter sends out his top gunman to stop the agent. Scott doesn't know that Kid Dynamite is waiting to kill him in his own evil way and looks as if he is doomed.

# BLOOD ON THE SKY

## Elliot Long

Will Hopkirk is settled for good with Diaglito's White Mountain Apaches and his beautiful Apache wife Sonseray. But then Diaglito is devastated when Tobias Hatch kills his young son, Choate. And white man's justice outrages Diaglito when it finds Hatch not guilty. The war chief vows that white man's blood must spill to satisfy the wrong done to him and his people. Now Hopkirk must choose where his loyalties lie, as the frontier erupts into a rage of violence.

# SHOWDOWN AT DANE'S BEND

## Jack Holt

Sam Limbo, innocent but jailed for murder, is forced to remain in Dane's Bend, a powder-keg town. The townsfolk are awaiting the arrival of the notorious Donovan brothers, intent on avenging the killing of the youngest Donovan. The brothers have a big interest in the bank which, with a secret stash, has taken on hired private security. Limbo breaks out of jail, but returns, lured by the marshal's daughter. And it's Limbo who saves the town that wanted to hang him.